Muc

Guide

to Capturing
The Latter-day
Soul

To the Anderson Family!
Let the Savior calm your
storms!

'13

Muckwhip's Guide to Capturing The Latter-day Soul

The Inside Scoop for Teens, Missionaries, and Families
on Avoiding the Pits and Snares of the Enemy

by

Chris Heimerdinger

Heimerdinger Entertainment

This is a work of fiction, and the views expressed herein are the sole responsibility of the author. Likewise, certain characters, places, and incidents are the product of the author's imagination, and any resemblance to actual persons, living or dead, or actual events or locales, is entirely coincidental.

Muckwhip's Guide to Capturing the Latter-day Soul

Published by Heimerdinger Entertainment

Cover design copyright © 2012 by Rachael Gibson

ISBN: 978-0-9708343-4-8

Printed in the United States of America
Year of first printing: 2012

For Gordon

You know who you are, Brother Jones,
and what you generously contributed,
so don't pretend otherwise.

I'd also like to offer profound appreciation to my wife, Emily, for sticking by me through my multitudinous ADDs, OCDs, and ASAPs. Thanks also to Marianne Olsen and Brenda Wright for their tireless and *voluntary* proofing services. Particular thanks also belongs to Rachel Ann Nunes for her kindness and online expertise. Also deserving of sincere appreciation is my on-call computer guru, John Weeks. I must thank BJ Rowley for his meticulous typesetting and Rachael Gibson for her creative and timely cover. Finally, I am indebted to Rebecca Fuller for a critical and life-saving last-minute suggestion.

Oh! and for this particular book, I should also thank every earthly soul I've ever met—in every variety of circumstances—since you were, and continue to be, an infinite source of inspiration.

"*There are two equal and opposite errors into which our race can fall about the devils. One is to disbelieve in their existence. The other is to believe, and to feel an excessive and unhealthy interest in them.*"

C. S. Lewis

HOW IT CAME ABOUT
(more or less)

Odd the things one can find when spending too much time on the computer.

More than a decade ago as I was attempting to research an answer to a particularly profound and vexing question put to me by a dedicated fan of my novels (I think it was as to whether Mr. Spock would be more appropriately called Brother Spock if the planet Vulcan converted to the gospel) when my internet connection unexpectedly shut down. As usual, the timing was quite bad. I'd delved into the web so deep that I felt sure I was on the brink of unearthing secrets heretofore unknown in the temporal universe. Suddenly *whammo!* Bill Gates' exasperating acerebral infrastructure (Windows) turned against me. Only this time I didn't maintain my usual cool and composed demeanor. I uttered a mild expletive (I think it was "pickle chips!"), whacked the monitor, and slammed my fist on the keyboard. It was then that I discovered that my connection hadn't been entirely severed. Well, perhaps my *normal* connection had been snipped, but somehow I had tapped into another kind of connection—another dimension of the World Wide Web. What appeared on my screen is the correspondence that follows.

I promptly saved the material to disk, after which my computer utterly fried, sparks exploded from the tower, the screen darkened, and my house lights flickered. Sadly, I lost the entire text of my next "Tennis Shoes" book (which certainly explains any untimely delays) but somehow I'd managed to extract this lone file.

I have therefore determined to reproduce the material here exactly as it first appeared, with the exception of a few spelling corrections. (Devils just can't seem to accurately spell words like *celestial* or *eternal*. The letters are always intermixed with exclamation points, dashes, and pound signs so that it looks more like a curse word.) I can't be certain if what I've discovered is evidence that Hell communicates via emails (or rather, h-mails) or if what I've tapped into is some sort of diabolical archive. I can't even say if this archive is complete. I have no idea of the identity of the living mortals referenced in the text—although I sense I may have met them a thousand times. Or seen them in the mirror. Finally, I'm no closer now to solving the mystery of how my computer was able to generate it.

I really must purchase a better filtering service . . .

(For a more sober, stuffy, clinical, and only marginally more logical explanation, read the Author's Foreward. But only if you have a tendency to take things *wayyy* too literally or are the type who never wearies of watching paint dry.)

C.H.

AUTHOR'S FOREWARD

This book was a long time in coming. Thirteen years, to be exact.

The first draft was finished in the year 2000. This latest manuscript is only a brush-up and slight retooling of that original version. I didn't publish it at the time because the concept seemed to cause my publisher serious conniptions. "Say that again, Chris: A book where *devils* are the main characters? A story told entirely from a *devil's* point of view?" The pallor on their faces was eminently apparent, despite the foreknowledge of other famous works that have explored similar themes. Some of these books and plays have existed for decades—even centuries—penned by such masters as Christopher Marlow, John Milton, Johann von Goethe, and C.S. Lewis. The object of such manuscripts was never to publicize or promote "devilry." Instead, they were meticulous efforts to educate us on the workings of the diabolical mind, to expose tactics that the adversary might employ to tempt and destroy us.

Thirteen years ago my publisher felt the LDS people were not ready for such a book. After all, who understands better than Latter-day Saints the reality of such evil and its persistent influences? Even today, whenever this subject is reluctantly discussed, we are well advised to treat it delicately and with healthy respect.

The best-known book with a similar theme is, without a doubt, C.S. Lewis's 1942 classic *The Screwtape Letters*. Unfortunately, I must admit that I've never read this volume. One might think I avoided it so as not to duplicate specific motifs from Lewis's "hellish" universe. The truth is that I first encountered the book when I was very young (high school? junior high?) and it simply could not hold my attention. Since that time I've read *other* books and articles by C. S. Lewis, and I can proudly call him one of my literary heroes. Still, I never worked my way back around to a consumption of *Screwtape*. Maybe now that my book is complete, I'll try again. Or maybe not. Perhaps only if my ego needs a good drubbing or I'm overcome by some masochistic need to feel put in my place as an intellectual and creative inferior. On most days such a need does not occur.

Thus, any similarities between *Screwtape* and *Muckwhip* are unintentional or coincidental. *Muckwhip* is neither a sequel nor a prequel. It must stand on its own. The original impetus for writing these "h-mails" was my conviction that, as a Latter-day Saint, the fullness of the Restored Gospel might offer me insights of unique importance. A silly presumption, I know, but I couldn't stop myself. I'm entirely cognizant of the challenge—and audacity—of thinking my little book can compare with other masterpieces. My hope is that such works can simply co-exist.

For readers sitting so low in elevation that the point of this book flies over their heads, let me state succinctly that it is fictional. There is nothing funny or entertaining about *real* demons. I won't even use that term. I much prefer "devil" and all the stereotypical images it conjures. Muckwhip is a *fictional* devil. No, he's not a creature with horns and a pronged tail. He's more like a cog or widget in a vast and dizzying corporate morass.

Everything in this book is symbolic and metaphorical. Instead of Milton's "fiery pit," I envisioned Hell as a sort of "dog-eat-dog" totalitarian bureaucracy, its occupants forever consumed by self-importance and personal advancement, gleefully eager to see discredit, demotion, and punishment fall upon even their closest colleagues. Yet on the surface everything is quite cordial, with frequent expressions of endearment and sugar-coated tributes to a job well done. Muckwhip is the epitome of such phoniness: witty, sagacious, and charmingly pompous. But make no mistake, beneath the crust he is lethally vicious and *always* self-serving.

Muckwhip's current rank is "Viceroy of Vice." His assignment is to oversee the myriad of tempters assigned to destroy members of the Church of Jesus Christ of Latter-day Saints. In his "h-mails," Muckwhip carefully mentors a neophyte imp named Frogknot on his favorite methods of corrupting individual "Targets." In Frogknot's case, his Target is a young man named Stuart Hansen.

One bit of symbolism that seemed apropos was the idea that Hell's objective in capturing souls is to provide livestock who will eventually become food. A devil's appetite can *also* be gratified by consuming other devils. This notion seemed relevant. After all, what is a devil if not a being whose unquenchable yearning is to draw all weaker beings inside itself?

The point of this book is not to encourage anyone to dwell upon the dreary realities of Hell, and I certainly hope that no one approaches me to ask if this is what I really believe Hell is like. My intent is to explore a few of our most conspicuous vulnerabilities in a way that is often lighthearted, sometimes deadly serious. Unfortunately, many of the weaknesses and foibles that are discussed I relate to only too well. Therefore, the reverse psychology is likely directed right back at me. I only hope others may also relate.

In reading these h-mails, always remember that a devil is a liar. Nothing Muckwhip says should be assumed to be true, even from his own point of view. Whatever Muckwhip welcomes, we ought to dread. Readers should view these h-mails as if they have just obtained the opposing team's playbook or the secret correspondence of an enemy spy. The purpose of this book is not to learn about devils, but that perhaps, through the eyes of a devil named Muckwhip, we might learn a thing or two about ourselves.

Chris Heimerdinger

1

From: "Muckwhip" <muckwhip@waydownbelow.hel>

To: <frogknot@waydownbelow.hel>

Subject: welcome!

MY DEAR FROGKNOT

Well done, my brightest and most promising apprentice!

It is with deepest pride that I congratulate you upon your current assignment. Welcome to the team! As you've likely heard, I've had my eye on you for quite some time. Such raw talent! Such promise! If only all of my recruits from the Institute of Advanced Temptation showed as much potential for exquisite, old-fashioned nastiness as you. Honestly, the overall quality of hirelings that ol' Headmaster Foggobblin has dropped into my lap of late has been despicable. I usually end up shipping them off for a "refresher course" in one of our more brutal Re-education Camps. Or else serving them as a side dish, *àla mode*, at one of our annual banquets.

But don't let this intimidate you. I'm sure that you, my newest son, are a cut above the average fiend. In fact, I saw to it that you were drafted into my department because I knew that you would never, *ever*, in your wildest nightmares even *think* of letting me down. Not you, my dear friend. You, Frogknot, as I've oft told my friends and associates here in the Lower Realms, are the Apple of My Eye, unlike other apprentices, whom I now confess I never saw as anything more than the Apple on My Plate.

As you are no doubt aware from all of the pamphlets I've over-nighted to your P.O. box, the success of our operation is of the highest priority to our infernal father. (Yes, I realize he's only our *step*father, but we nevertheless pay him the highest homage, fully aware of the consequences if we do not. I've tried my *darndest* to uppercase the I and F in his title, but can't seem to convince my word precessing program to comply. The same difficulty emerges whenever I attempt to *lower*case the names or titles of the Opposition, Archenemy, or His Firstborn Son. No matter how assiduously I try to make these names lowercase, my spellchecker simply will not cooperate! Ugg! The frustration!)

You can be sure the critical nature of our mission is why they gave *me* charge over the whole devil-awful department some years back. The two previous heads became, of necessity, "headless" as a result of their mournful failures. I inherited an ugly situation indeed. It's taken every ounce of my prowess as a Tempter First Class to steer things back onto a proper course. A 180° turnaround is now imminent.

Still, I am always in need of gifted junior tempters like yourself to drive the final nails into the Organization's coffin. Yes, that's what we call it in these precincts—the "Organization." In your correspondence you must never refer to it as anything else. I've always rather liked that word, relating as closely as it does with words like "organism" or "organ" (an instrument whose creepy chords I loathe with every fiber of my being).

You most certainly will never refer to it as anything even remotely like its official title—the Church of Something Something of Latter-day Whatever. If you must call it anything, please employ the old standby term—"Mormons."

We've successfully propagandized most of humanity into applying that term, preferably with a sneer. Thus, continue standard usage of that name, thus obscuring any association it might have with our Archenemy.

My predecessor, through sheer stupidity, briefly forgot the value of this label. He allowed some individuals in educated circles to stop employing it, including (Hell help us!) the mainstream media. These people are traditionally our most enduring allies in promoting this moniker. Not to worry. I am confident that I will reignite old habits. The term *Mormon* will, if I have my way, once again dominate all other appellations.

Nevertheless, as far as you and I are concerned, I much prefer the sterile term "Organization." Not only for the sake of poetics, but because it continually reminds us that our principal objective is to turn the whole confounded thing into something more accurately described as the "*Dis*-organization."

I was somewhat alarmed when my secret informers told me that you shuddered and paled after opening your assignment envelope, learning that you would be joining this department. I hope this has nothing to do with all those unhelpful rumors so commonly repeated at the Institute. You know the ones I mean: Those who describe this as the most formidable and distasteful department in all of the Community of Contention. Such rumors generally adopt one of two angles: either they speak of vast concourses of devils—tormented, wounded, bruised, and battle worn from incessant confrontations with the Opposition—or they claim that it teems with tempters who loll about, twiddling their thumbs, helpless, suffocated and nearly self-combusting out of sheer boredom as they are prevented from mounting effective attacks. Kindly put both notions in the boondocks of your imagination.

Though I confess our work is at times challenging, it's not nearly as burdensome as some have whispered. If all facts were properly publicized, this would assuredly be the most coveted assignment in all the Lower Realms. There is no commission you might have received whose rewards are more delightful or whose Feasts of Souls are more satisfying. Nothing, I repeat, *nothing* goes down more smoothly than a well-seasoned Mormon.

But surely you already knew this. I will therefore conclude, Frogknot, that your shudder of frame and blanch of hue were inspired not because of unfortunate rumors, but because you learned that you would soon be working for *me*. In which case, I am duly flattered.

I anticipate your arrival A.S.A.P. Target 120-16A-44M is in dire need of your attentions.

Your Supreme Superintendent,
MUCKWHIP

Part I:

AGAINST YOUTH

2

From: "Muckwhip" <muckwhip@waydownbelow.hel>
To: <frogknot@waydownbelow.hel>
Subject: you made it!

MY DEAR FROGKNOT,

Just a note to express my rapturous pleasure at how well you are adjusting to your duties. I realize it's not quite the position you may have anticipated—certainly nothing so important as to merit an increase in benefits or privileges. Still, it does qualify you for enrollment in our department's dental plan. This should come in quite handy as soon as our inevitable victory is declared and we finally receive a body of flesh and bone, along with a full magazine of teeth. In the meantime, rest assured that you are fully covered.

Even if your first Target, 17-year-old Mr. Stuart Hansen, has every appearance of becoming an easy candidate for consumption, do not allow yourself to wax overconfident. He certainly appears typical of so many young males—tall, dark-eyed, cocky, ambitious, terrified of females, and infinitely curious about every worldly and forbidden thing. We are aggrieved that he still maintains any kind of association with the Organization, albeit such connections deteriorate almost daily.

As I'm sure you've already realized, he hails from a wonderfully dysfunctional family. His father hasn't darkened the chapel door for eight happy years, thanks to Sputcurse, the fiend currently assigned to precipitate daddy's downfall. The primary issue that led to his father's antipathy toward the Organization is actually quite amusing. Sputcurse deftly took advantage of a doctrinal dispute that took place in one of their so-called priesthood meetings. It regarded whether or not a stalwart Saint should view sporting events on Sunday. The fireworks were spangled and lovely. We successfully planted an offense in the minds of virtually every contributor in the room. By the time the incident was, for the most part, forgotten, Sputcurse had nimbly persuaded the father to concoct a dozen additional rationales for not attending. We fully expect your Target to reap copious benefits from his dad's example.

His mother, unfortunately, remains stubbornly active in the Organization. However, her influence has been largely neutralized since her hold over the boy is predicated heavily upon besieging him with guilt. We've urged her to incorporate some delightful methods for making her son feel keenly inferior for his shortcomings. Thus, the boy is developing a natural sense of repugnance for everything his mother holds dear.

What makes us most uneasy is your Target's persistent attendance at Sunday services, and particularly his midweek youth activities. Expend every effort to promptly countermand such practices. I'll have Sputcurse assist you by smuggling into his father's thoughts additional weekend plans for father/son hunting and fishing excursions. Even if your boy presently attends church only to please his mum, a continual weekly reminder of Organizational principals could eventually, inadvertently, become etched onto his psyche. Oh, he might perceive as irrelevant all of that tripe about life and salvation now, but patterns may still formulate in the back of his noodle, cropping up in later life and encouraging him to seek some kind of spiritual renaissance. This must be repressed at all cost. The earlier we can conclusively sever his ties to the Organization the better! And the less likely it will be that *any* unseemly nugget of so-called wisdom from some fireside sermon or a random lyric from a Primary ditty can become entrenched in his subconscious.

As I'm sure was beaten into your brain during your first semester at the Institute, our best opportunity for capturing souls is ever—and always will be—when a Target is a teenager. If your experience was anything like mine, they pummeled you with this precept to near delirium every hour of the day. (Such happy memories! I must blot a tear.)

Now is the ideal time to ingrain in your pollywog all of the twisted habits, attitudes, and opinions that will ensure his eventual extermination. If you exercise due diligence, these vices will enslave him well into his days of octogenarian oblivion. For example, if you wait until your Target is in his late twenties before tempting him with provocative images, narcotics, or self-abuse, you might never arrive at square one. Ensnare him while he's young, my wily apprentice! Repeat this directive on a daily basis. We must fasten such bindings while he still regards himself as invincible, indestructible, and perceives that he has oodles of time to untangle all of our tethers and snarls. At this age he is like wet clay. If we remain persistent (and we always do), we can transform him in later years into whatever breed of debauched creature we desire.

I should warn you, however. We are not the only ones who understand the critical nature of a subject's adolescent years. The Archenemy knows it too. He wants to own your Target almost as much as we do. Certainly not more. He couldn't possibly want them more. *Why* does He want them? We're still not sure. Since He doesn't eat them, it makes no sense. All that nonsense about bringing to pass their immortality and eternal life for His own joy and glory is a load of indigestible dung. It just doesn't compute. What's in it for Him? We've tried since time memorial to discover His *true* intentions, deploying our most sophisticated accountants and actuaries, but to no avail. Analysis remains ongoing.

In any case, be watchful of every seemingly insignificant artifice that the Opposition might employ. As we've all learned from sad experience, it's often when Targets are teenagers that the Archenemy drafts His most dynamic recruits. That Smith scalawag from the nineteenth century being the most wretched example. Oh, what a terrible loss to have allowed that one to slip through our fingers! I was assisting in another department at the time or I'm sure the whole fiasco would have been nipped in the bud far more effectively. The incompetent fiends in charge of him were convinced, despite repeated warnings from the Central Office, that the Opposition would wait until Joe was much older and had made his mark in the world, perhaps as a famous politician or popular itinerant preacher. Oh, such wretched idiocy! The Opposition struck when the boy was a mere whelp! Fourteen years old! Any imbecile should have realized that the Archenemy would strike while the pollywog was still young and pliable. This allowed him to raise the lad to do things *His* way instead of the world's way (or in other words, *our* way.)

So as strange as it seems, the objectives of Heaven and Hell are surprisingly identical. We're both in the business of owning souls. We just happen to be a bit more honest and forthright about it: *We want to devour the little varmints!!!*

So beware, Frogknot, of all the tricks and schemes of the Opposition to secure the devotions of youth. And by all means remind your comrade, Trumpitch, to do all he can to silence his mother's ranting prayers in her son's behalf. If you read last week's newsletter, you'll remember that I gave these same instructions to each and every tempter in my department— STOP THOSE INFERNAL PRAYERS IN BEHALF OF THE YOUTH OF THE CHURCH! If I do not see a steady decline in such utterances immediately, I will be forced to reduce feast rations and require triple shifts on Halloween.

Your Affable Anchorman,
MUCKWHIP

3

From: "Muckwhip" <muckwhip@waydownbelow.hel>
To: <frogknot@waydownbelow.hel>
Subject: trifecta

MY DEAR FROGKNOT,

I received your initial bi-weekly report, and I must say that your overuse of servile phrases like "extraordinary skill set," "wicked wit," and "imperious intelligence" in describing my attributes are little more than vain and obvious attempts at kissing up. It reminded me of the tail waggings of an abused puppy. In short, I liked it very much.

As you have asked my opinion regarding "the best angles of attack" on a Mormon teenager, I offer my standard threefold retort: social insecurity, the itch for independence, and boredom. Actually, these are successful fronts for enfeebling *any* adolescent, but there are certain nuances that will make your Target especially vulnerable.

With regard to social insecurity, your boy is a sucker for public opinion. It's almost laughable. Like all youth, he believes upwards of *everything* he is ever told about himself— particularly by peers. At this time of his life more than any other he is an absolute slave to fad, fashion, and females. Oh, he may consider himself an independent thinker—and should ever be *encouraged* to see himself as such. But during no other phase is he more paranoid about anything he might do or say that might earn the classification of being "uncool" (or any of its fashionable synonyms). This he'll deny, but we are not so naïve. Tragically oversensitive, you will find him willing to do virtually anything in that oh-so-nebulous quest to "belong." Of course, some youngsters will seek refuge within their families to circumvent such tripe, but not your boy. Thanks to the disharmony we've long cultivated in that environment, his "home" is the *last* place he wants to be.

Your object, therefore, is to entangle him in just the right cliques, surround him with just the right friends—i.e., allies for our cause who can bend him to believe that any moral or virtue he learned in a religious setting is painfully stifling and embarrassing. The Organization itself must be viewed as uncool. Or in more incisive terms: bigoted, parochial, and asphyxiating. Its leaders are imbeciles; its programs intended to pester. Hypocrites are ubiquitous. If he adopts just one of these perspectives, your task becomes all the more elementary.

Also, such efforts neatly segue into his second vulnerability—the need for independence. Ah, but this is a fertile arena for gaining advantage! Your Target is predisposed to wean himself not only from the influence of parents but from *all* adults. He believes he *is* an adult, sharper and keener, without all the unavoidable impediments of Alzheimer's, which (as his personal observations suggest) begins its onset on all human beings over the age of 30. Persist in reminding him that he deserves all of the freedoms and status that adulthood implies. Milk this to its maximum advantage. Buttress it. Ennoble it. Let anyone who questions his post-pubescence find themselves at the pinnacle of his black list. He must question every precept he's ever learned. This, in and of itself, is not precisely our objective, because often the things he questions are his own quixotic conclusions and faulty worldviews. No, no, these we must keep intact. Whenever a young Target finds himself in a state of hostility or disgruntlement about the place wherein life has planted him, we are infinitely freer to entice him with our more corrupting philosophies.

Finally, exploit young Stuart's incurable tendency toward boredom. This is the *ad nauseam* lament of all teenagers. Oh, how they whine about it! Throughout their mortal probation they have held fast the opinion that it was the inflexible responsibility of others—parents, teachers, and every other pulchritudinous personality—to *entertain* them. From infancy they've sought out fresh and unique stimulations to keep them engaged. Now in the bloom of adolescence your Target is starting to inquire, "Is this it? Is there nothing more to life? Just pain, trials, and loneliness?" Your answer is always and resoundingly "yes!" A gazillion times "YES!"

In past eras, of course, we haven't had the luxury of tending to such groveling self-indulgence. Most parents kept their nippers occupied by a solid day's work. It was a matter of survival. But this is an age of affluence. Your Target is as spoiled as summer compost. I assure you, however, he sees the situation exactly the opposite, and this is good. Continue to let the world fall short of his expectations. Encourage him to internalize deep, heart-wrenching disappointment in people and principles. Drive him inconsolably *berserk* with boredom! Then strike with the obvious solution—SIN. And only the most delicious varieties. This, he will discover—with all the curiosity of a kitten jostling a ball of yarn—is his *only* unexplored outlet of stimulation. Through attrition, you will convince him that without it, he may shrivel up and die. How I delight in watching the progression! It's so basic. So academic. So enthralling, I insist upon popcorn.

Focus upon these three strategies as your staging grounds for every sortie. Make it a rotating "trifecta" of assault. If human history and experience tells us anything, young Mr. Hansen will find himself thoroughly defenseless. You'll have an entire smorgasbord of temptations at your fingertips. Do not neglect a single course!

Your Malignant Master Chef,
MUCKWHIP

4

From: "Muckwhip" <muckwhip@waydownbelow.hel>
To: <frogknot@waydownbelow.hel>
Subject: opposite sex

MY DEAR FROGKNOT,

I'm mildly impressed with the progress you are making in regards to your Target's interest in sex. The last imp in charge of Mr. Hansen made precious little headway in this arena. That's why I had him join me for dinner some months back. An unappetizing topic, I assure you.

Let me tell you where your predecessor went awry. He focused so much energy on destroying Mr. Hansen's self-esteem that the boy was convinced he wasn't the least bit attractive to females. We got away with this strategy when he was a lanky, pimple-faced squirt. But when he outgrew that phase last summer, your predecessor should have adjusted his tactics. In August we had a perfect opportunity to thrust him into the arms of a girl with the standards of a sewer grate, but because of issues of self-esteem, he didn't even realize she was flirting! No, the low esteem thing became a colossal overkill.

As you must be aware, there are few sins that deaden the soul to the promptings of the Archenemy's Spirit more than sexual immorality. To our infinite credit, we've exponentially multiplied our success in this category with each successive generation—and we have no anticipation that we will ever lose ground again. I've not seen our infernal father so ecstatic since the orgy-fests of ancient Rome. Who could have imagined such a succulent harvest? Only our ignoble father. Hear! Hear!

Our strides worldwide have also provided much fruit among the members of the Organization, especially (but not exclusively) its younger adherents. Our new crop of libertines is younger and younger every year. Youth of the new century accept no constraints. In fact, they are *obsessed* with the subject. And not just because of hormones and other contributors. We've made sex the preeminent focus of teenage repartee, for both boys *and* girls. Even before your Target frolicked off on his first official "date" last Spring, he knew more about the methodology and minutiae of the subject than many persons of the previous generation fathomed after twenty years of marriage. And not because Stuart made any particular effort to research the matter. For pity's sake, we've introduced the most urbane perversities into their most common vernacular! Techniques and variations are batted back and forth in the dialogue of television sitcoms. They command the rhetoric of internet blogs. They're maximized in the prose of best-selling fiction, entangled in the lyrics of mainstream music, dissected on the nightly news, and bandied about by patrons and employees at the neighborhood mini-mart. The fables and fabrications of sex resound from the highest mountaintops! They monopolize magazine covers. Wink back from restroom walls. Intimacy is anything *but* intimate! It is *omnipresent!* If any boy or girl isn't savvy to the facts of life by the age of six, the teenybopper lives in a grotto! Needless to say, we've been grooming Mr. Hansen for a fatal plunge into this inescapable net his entire life. You need only employ a single finger to poke him off the cliff and into the abyss.

First things first. In case you haven't noticed, Stuart Hansen has far too much respect for the opposite sex. The other day he asked a feminist classmate for her honest opinion regarding a woman's role in the workforce. Never mind how the girl launched into an exquisite harangue about how no woman should have to submit to the slavery of marriage or child rearing. That was all well and good. What bothered me, and what should have pestered *you*, was the overall *respect* that he showed her. Patiently listening. Honestly striving to empathize. It was *nauseating!* Such behavior must be undermined at once. Your boy will be educated to see females as little more than lollipops to satisfy his lust and gratification. In the past this approach was reserved primarily for males. However, the inroads we've made with transferring this attitude onto women in recent years have surpassed all expectations. Whole training manuals have been rewritten to accommodate new strategies and opportunities.

Discourage your Target from ever believing he might cultivate an actual *friendship* with these creatures. Repeat to him over and over that women are incomprehensible. They are inferior. Self-absorbed. Fickle. Secretive. Conspiratorial. Unpredictable. In short, they are the *enemy*. And as the enemy, they *must be conquered*. Every relationship with a female must be seen as a conquest. Not necessarily sexual at first (although spontaneous opportunities should never go unexploited). In the beginning let it simply be a matter of who has the upper hand. Who has control. His entire courtship experience in youth is merely a rehearsal stage for mastering all the potential means of manipulating women. I promise you, the compulsion for control will carry over into marriage. If we're persistent, it should emerge in *every* relationship with the opposite sex in every facet of his life.

The moment he starts to think that he might treat these mealworms as equals, partners, or mutual companions, the battle is turning against you. Control (I cannot apply this word too often) should perpetually be at the forefront of his mind. Even if he gives in to these petty females from time to time, it's only for the greater good of establishing ever-increasing control. This should build and build until he finally squashes her. Or until she squashes *him*. It really doesn't matter. Just as long as somebody is being squashed. After all, we're in the squashing business.

I hope you're up-to-date on the current fixation among teenagers in the Organization regarding how far they can "go" on a date and still consider themselves "worthy." *Your* answer to this question is invariably *all the way.* But initially you must convince your Target that this is an insoluble quandary, much like astrophysics or quantum mechanics. Far too complex for ordinary human apprehension. Keep him over-intellectualizing. If you allow him to make it a *spiritual* question, the jig is up.

He'll recognize, to our perpetual frustration, that by imploring the aid of his infuriating "gift" he can realize the correct answer at any given moment, and that no internal disputation was ever required. It is an atrocious epiphany. The more you can get him to discuss detailed fantasies and fables with his friends (*never* with adults or Organizational leaders), the more likely you will be to persuade him that the sky's the limit. There's always an ample supply of fools who will proclaim that he/she can go as far as they desire without going "all the way." I love the logic that boundaries vary for various personalities; that some young salamanders can cuddle and smooch for hours without the interference of expanding temptation while others are inclined to plunge into immorality after a single peck. Your boy will invariably want to test himself to identify to which category he belongs. Then he'll keep testing himself. And keep testing himself. All the while you must reinforce the subterfuge: "Yes, I'm still in control . . . Yup, still in control . . ." It's all a wicked, wonderful illusion, of course.

With each successive notch *we're* the ones who seize greater control. I can assure you that if you pursue this pattern of attack you will enjoy countless hours of sidesplitting entertainment as you lead your Target by the proboscis through all the stages of gray to the most stygian blacks.

What your boy doesn't realize—what he must *never* realize—is that for us this is all a sort of race against time. The Opposition has given them all of these drives and instincts naturally—deliberately. Now don't snicker. It's absolutely true. Cross my heart and hope to live. The Archenemy's object is far more cunning than you might realize. If your Target disciplines these drives while in his youth, the result can be catastrophic. I'm thoroughly disgusted every time I ponder two of these jackanapes genuflecting across the altar inside one of those impenetrable temples, wholly clean and poisonously pure because of our devastating failures.

So in our race against time, it's essential that we get them dating, courting, "hanging out" and "hooking up" with one another as soon as possible. Eight is not too soon. Nine is adequate. Ten is tolerable. Eleven is acceptable. Twelve is tremendous! Thus we'll have every chance to send their natural drives spiraling out of control. The sooner we can entice them to advance from hand-holding to kissing to more advanced stimulations, the sooner we can smush them like cockroaches and grind them into the pavement.

Oh, and remember, once you snag any kind of hook into Mr. Hansen's hubris, keep him physically as far away from bishops and other Organizational pests as humanly possible. These people are *anathema* to everything we seek to accomplish. Inundate your Target with fear and loathing over any type of confrontation with these imperious prudes. Remind him that his bishop is his neighbor—just a few doors down the avenue. If he succumbs to some kind of embarrassing, soul-crushing confessional, he will still be forced to walk despondently past this person's driveway every day. *Every single day!* And every day, behind his bishop's insipid smile, will abide the flavor of bile. Reinforce to your Target that his bishop cannot possibly forget the awful particulars of his abhorrent admissions. Magnify in your Target's mind the falsehood that there is no confession in history quite as reprehensible as his, certainly nothing that approaches such a nauseating and execrable character. Blockade any perception of the resuscitating, meliorating power associated with a bishop's mantle. Plug his ears. Sing "fa-la-la-la-la!" as loudly as your lungs can bray. One meddling bishop can spoil an entire buffet. Ofttimes we must begin again at square one. What an egregious loss!

Can you introduce your boy to a nice girl? That is, to an ally for our cause? Preferably a temptress whose strings we already yank and draw like a marionette? In addition, I insist, Frogknot, that after you achieve this feat, please, *please* encourage your Target to overcome just a sliver of his shyness and insecurity. Not too much. There is a subtle balance here. He must remain moderately reluctant. This is how our siren will exercise her ultimate supremacy. It's always better if your boy believes this may, in fact, be the only girl who will ever truly fall for him.

In the meantime, keep stimulating his curiosity. I was pleased that you managed to entice him (albeit subliminally) into rooting for the hero and heroine to commit an immoral act in a recent episode of his favorite prime-time drama. I'd love to ogle oodles of these kinds of incongruities. But keep such lapses of logic buried in his subconscious for now. We certainly wouldn't want him to recognize our gradual and inescapable progression.

Your Imperial Inquisitor,
MUCKWHIP

5

From: "Muckwhip" <muckwhip@waydownbelow.hel>

To: <frogknot@waydownbelow.hel>

Subject: hyperventilating

MY DEAR FROGKNOT,

I read with grave concern the postscript at the end of your latest h-mail admitting that your Target was invited into his bishop's office to discuss whether he might be interested in serving a mission. It is with extraordinary effort that I retain my composure. Are you really so ADDLEHEADED as to think that this tidbit deserves no more acknowledgment than an INFANTILE POSTSCRIPT?!

Even more disturbing is your passive mention that because you were unable to penetrate the premises you're not entirely certain what was discussed. I realize, Frogknot, that you are new to this post. Therefore I will allow myself only a few feeble hyperventilations and proceed to instruct you in my most patient and delicate manner, as befitting a father whose affections for his wayward spawn run so very deep.

Let's look at your most glaring oversight. Don't misunderstand me. It's not that I fail to grasp your strategy of making the Target *functionally* inactive in the Organization before he is *literally* inactive. I'm happy to learn that he doesn't croak a single note of any hymn during services. I'm pleased by his inclination to exchange texts with friends across the chapel, and particularly impressed that you have convinced him to loiter loquaciously in the hallway during much of Sunday School and Priesthood. But don't you think you should have encouraged him to lollygag at the opposite end of the edifice instead of the very foyer where his bishop would most certainly spot him? This is just another reason why it is critical that you extricate him from that building *altogether!*

What's done is done. Let us now assess the damage. In truth, what was discussed in the bishop's cubby is not nearly as important as the posture that Mr. Hansen exhibited when he emerged. Did the boy appear crestfallen, perhaps offended that his spiritual leader might even *suggest* something as outlandish as tracting for two-years in some vermin-infested precinct like Bolivia or Bulgaria? Were your Target's features cloaked in indifference or doubt, convinced that he could never in a million years prepare himself for such a grueling assignment? Did he look dismally, viscerally ashamed, mortified that his sins—his very *musings* of sin!—have made him wholly unfit for the Archenemy's services? Any such sentiment could be warped to our advantage.

What would concern me most is if he came out of that office looking preoccupied, expectant, even ebullient; a tear in his eye, confident and calm. This would confirm that the Archenemy's Spirit, which kept you at bay, did His dirty work. Such a prospect could not be more serious. It would demand immediate retaliation, potentially forcing us to deploy the heavy artillery. But before we overreact and blow a hole in our annual budget, remember that a great deal can still be attained by a skillful application of the *power of suggestion.* Subtle prods, well timed, can suffocate any budding desire to enlist in the Opposition's pimple-faced army.

For instance, can you plant in Mr. Hansen's subconscious the tidbit that his bishop is really cut from the same cloth as his nagging mother? Can you convince him that the entire Organization is nothing but an interfering taskmaster? If he can come to believe that it's the *Church* that stands in the way of true happiness and contentment, ah, Frognot, what a beautiful thing!

Two years!—to a young man like Stuart Hansen this is nothing short of an eternity! Although a modern young man generally operates on the assumption of time's prodigious abundance, selfish tendencies can quickly morph this perspective. Time suddenly becomes a priceless commodity. Remind him of the opportunity cost, of chances that may never come again. Scream to his consciousness that if two full years (twenty-four months! one-hundred and five weeks! seven-hundred and thirty days!) are sacrificed at this precious interval, his lifelong dreams may never reach fruition. Deliver to his imagination a hovering vision of his worldly objectives: money, love, pleasure, fame—whatever ambition works! Choose one or a combination of many and *hammer, hammer, hammer* them home!

Fortunately, we still possess a certain incontrovertible advantage. Your Target has never claimed to have a so-called "testimony" of the Organization, its prophets, or its doctrines. Therefore, you are free to play upon his sense of moral and intellectual superiority. He's already snugly ensconced in apathy. He considers church the most tedious three hours of the week. With the slightest nudge, you can turn apathy into antipathy. Can you help his bishop's remarks resonate like a chorus of clichés? Can you prompt him to adopt this same attitude with regard to what is said in every religious service he attends? Emphasize the repetitive, inane, chalkboard-screeching nature of what he hears. Amplify his disgust for vapid phrases like "I *knowwww* this Church is true," or "Bless this food that it may give us nourishment and strength," or "Help us to apply these principles in our daily lives," etc., etc. Surely your boy can be made to see that most of the Archenemy's adherents repeat such phrases with little or no forethought. They might as well simultaneously plan the evening meal or ponder the sagacity of SpongeBob SquarePants. Let your Target marvel at the absence of creativity, the lack of conscious effort. I assure you, he will start to feel quite superior—precipitously higher than the level of these chattering parakeets. If he ever considers that an individual's devotion or testimony is sincere, whisper that this is only because the poor sucker has been brainwashed by a lifetime of mythological mishmash. Never, *never*, let your Target conclude that anyone out there actually *knows* anything. They may *think* they know. They may even "believe" it. But never could a man conceivably *know* something so sublime, so non-existential.

The concept itself—literally *knowing* that something is true—invokes an incurable curiosity, leading far too many to exert a genuine effort to discover if such abstract, intangible tripe can actually be discerned! Remind him that of *course* no one knows the unknowable. The very notion denounces the world's vast compendium of common sense! What is faith against the intensity of so many billions of agnostic and disbelieving voices? (Voices, by the way, that we are obliged and eager to amplify!) In the face of such a cacophony, faith most assuredly fails, becoming a wallowing, blushing, and helpless thing. Or so it will appear to most. Or so it must *always* appear.

But if, by some strange aberration, Stuart Hansen ever shows symptoms of being deeply moved by sincere testimony, your strategy must turn on a dime. You must immediately emphasize all of the testifier's chinks and faults. For example, does this testimony bearer have a hair-trigger temper? Will he at the slightest provocation cut loose with some vile profanity?

Is he or she guilty in their past of any of our more malignant sins? Take advantage of every opportunity to expose a testifier as a flaming hypocrite. Even the way a testifier bites his nails, the obnoxiousness of his children, or even the poor quality of his automobile, can clinch the deal. You'd be surprised how quickly we can delude a Target into deciding that because a testifier cannot match his socks and his necktie, he couldn't *possibly* know whether a thing is true.

Above all else, do not allow Mr. Hansen to remotely consider petty promises regarding those who "lack wisdom." Dismiss with all fervency any effort he might pursue to make honest inquiries of the Archenemy. Oh, how I dread this underhanded ploy! Twist the very idea into a murkiness of abstractions, *abstractions*, ABSTRACTIONS! I realize this is much easier with older Targets. Your caterpillar isn't far enough removed from his years as a little child, when he still possessed all of the humility, faithfulness, and other nonsense that the Opposition constantly applauds as a superior state of being. Use this to your advantage. Don't let the Archenemy use it for His. With only the slightest prod, teenage humility can be transformed into "open-mindedness." For our purposes, this means that he'll swallow just about anything that he believes enhances his popularity, attractiveness, or sense of independence. To the Opposition it means that he can be prompted to seek spiritual guidance in all its simplicity and purity, which, I assure you, could damage our cause irreparably and invoke the wrath of every department in the Infernal Realms.

The older the Target, the easier it is to fog frank, straightforward interpretations of spiritual events. Things like, "What I felt was the result of something I ate," or "I *convinced* myself that I felt something only because I desperately *wanted* to feel it," or (my personal favorite) "What I felt was simply an aberration of the senses stimulated by a combination of natural physiological influences that may or may not have any relationship to spiritual phenomenon."

Unfortunately these interpretations do not work as well on teenagers. They're still far too accepting of data at face value. We haven't yet taught them to complicate things the way we like. If the Archenemy's Spirit elbows your boy, I fear he'll recognize the reality of the experience far too readily. This is why it is absolutely critical that you prevent him from ever making a serious, prayerful inquiry as to whether the Organization is true, whether what's-his-name is a prophet of God, or whether those gold plates translated by Mr. Smith are, in fact, scripture. And in your present case—*do not under any circumstances allow Mr. Hansen to ask whether or not he should serve a mission!*

If it is ever reported to me that such an inquiry was made, Frogknot, you will find no place of refuge in any recess of the Lower Realms. Expect swift and excruciating consequences.

Your Unwavering Employer,
MUCKWHIP

6

From: "Muckwhip" <muckwhip@waydownbelow.hel>
To: <frogknot@waydownbelow.hel>
Subject: nice work!

MY DEAR FROGKNOT,

I read your latest dispatch with sheer delight. I even faxed a copy of it to the Central Office, omitting, of course, your name wherever you naïvely credit yourself, and substituting my own.

But strictly between you and me, *well done!* Recent developments in young Mr. Hansen's life are ample proof of your abundant talents. I am happy to issue to you one credit toward solid advancement in the Department. You're well on your way, ol' chap. Only 999,999,999 credits to go.

I'm particularly impressed with the way you isolated your Target from any further attendance at church. *Touché!* For you to have capitalized upon the chance meeting in the school hallway betwixt your boy and the sensuous Miss Janielle Sessions was prime work indeed, reminiscent of my own early days as a tempter. We've already utilized Miss Sessions on several occasions with roaring success. Don't let those bohemian blue eyes or delicate pouting lips deceive you. She's cunningly calculating, ravenously self-serving and stupendously superficial. But in such an unconventional way that most of those who cross her path will contend that she's the most altruistic individual they've ever met!

Oh, I like her, Frogknot! (That is to say, I *hate* her, but you know what I mean.) She is consumed by vanity, smoldering with pride, and lascivious to the point of calling it a virtue. Best of all, with respect to your Target, she's highly persuasive in her defense of "personal freedom" and liberating oneself from the shackles of religion. I don't have to tell you how eager some of us are down here to one day sink our teeth into *that* one. What a flavor! What a crunch!

I'm certainly not surprised that it took mere minutes for Miss Session to reel him in so securely. She hit all the right buttons. Did she really try to flatter him over his musical finesse? Legions of us cackled out loud at *that* one. She knows perfectly well that his talents are appallingly mediocre, yet she soft-soaped him all the same.

I loved the way you instantly turned his attention to his pocketbook. One does not skimp while courting Miss Sessions. But you must always assure him that the results will be infinitely worth it. Was he really calling the classifieds just an hour after school dismissed? Oh, Frogknot, you are a subtle fiend! I especially enjoyed the twist you snuck into his psyche that he was not acquiring a job to woo Miss Sessions, but to potentially save money for a mission. Keep playing that angle. But be careful. Don't ever allow him to remotely believe it. It must remain purely a rationalization. Let it be the thing he tells his mother if she ever questions his judgment. Then we'll all watch with succulent pleasure as his illustrious female friend picks his pocket of every nickel, penny, and peso. In case you missed it in Miss Sessions' dossier, she prefers a suitor who drives no less than a Ford F-150. It would be well if you could stimulate your Target to make an investment that will strangle his finances well into his twenties, thus making even the idea of a mission a mathematical impossibility.

Finally, I'm profoundly pleased with your success at encouraging him to select a job that will force him to work Sundays. *Bravo!* You've topped my loftiest expectations, my miniscule myrmidon! At long last his ties to the Organization will be permanently amputated. And not a moment too soon!

I will point out, however, that the vast majority of credit still belongs to me. After all, *I* was the one who ordered your comrade, Grubworm, to elbow the owner of that computer game outlet (a man solidly under our thumb) to hire your boy on the spot. You see, I suspected that the delivery shop where he first interviewed might call back, allowing him the option of working Monday, Wednesday, and Friday. This would have done us no good at all. Still, I cannot overlook your important, albeit meager, contribution. I noticed that when the delivery shop *did* finally call, you whispered a wily reminder to your Target that the game store was offering an additional dime per hour. Nicely done!

Now watch, my dear Frogknot. Sit back and bask in the irony. Think of the hilarious explanation Mr. Hansen will shortly present to his mother: "But Mom, I'm working on Sunday to save for a mission! Isn't that what you *wanted?*" Ah, I must allow myself a satisfied sigh. There are few moments for us in Hell more mouth moistening than to hear any mortal—especially a teenager—maintain that he must break one commandment in order to keep another.

I anticipate that young Mr. Hansen will soon require far less attention. His destiny will be well in hand. I simply forewarn you not to fumble the ball. All that we've really done is inch open the door. Now we will begin cinching our strongest cords. I look forward with fervency to your next report.

Your Perfidious Patriarch,
MUCKWHIP

7

From: "Muckwhip" <muckwhip@waydownbelow.hel>
To: <frogknot@waydownbelow.hel>
Subject: the "gift"

MY DEAR FROGKNOT,

I'm disappointed that your Target did not fall into serious transgression during his initial rendezvous with Miss Sessions, but by no means discouraged. Certainly she did everything she could—immodest clothing, seductive hints, alluring body language. I'm afraid, Frogknot, you have just experienced your first setback as a result of that interfering mechanism known as *conscience*. No matter. It is only an ephemeral defeat. However, I must unfortunately revoke the single credit that you earned previously.

The fact is, Mr. Hansen is not fully prepared to exercise that galling "gift" confirmed upon him shortly after his watery dunk in the stake center's font. This "gift" is a far more terrifying adversary than neophyte fiends such as yourself can remotely fathom. It has cheated us out of countless victories, utilizing methods that are quite unsportsmanlike, employing the pointblank powers of the Opposition's arsenal. Our advantage is that after this "gift" is *bestowed* it must be *received*. This does not occur automatically. The Target has to *desire* it, seek for it, request it. Furthermore, it's only when your Target is humble and contrite (a rare condition indeed) and when he acknowledges his full dependence upon the Archenemy (a rarer condition still), that he can fully benefit from its power. Therefore, our opportunities to undermine this convoluted defense increase exponentially.

Like so many other teenagers in this intolerable Organization, Mr. Hansen doesn't even realize that he wields this power. Oh, he may realize it in some trifling, lubberly way. But he never much ponders it, and he *certainly* hasn't registered its staggering ramifications. I shudder to think what might have happened if you, a mere amateur, had been confronted by the intensity of such a ruthless juggernaut. Never mind. It was not detected.

What defeated you was that same slimy vicissitude promiscuously bestowed upon every human being ever born, religious and nonreligious, regardless of race, intelligence or culture. Members of the Organization call it the "Light of You-Know-Who." The rest of the world calls it "conscience" or "an innate sense of right and wrong," or they identify it with the name of a certain irritating cricket. You might have heard Headmaster Foggobblin at the Institute describe it as "the Opposition's first and feeblest line of defense." And so it is. Breaking through it is always accomplished by attrition—steady, relentless, and sure.

Your boy has never given any consideration to the idea of thought control. He's atrocious at it. He's already practiced many sins repeatedly in his imagination. He practices them in computer games and in an accruing and accelerating number of virtual reality mediums, committing murder and mayhem at will, relishing such acts over and over, again and again, without reprisal or consequence—or so he thinks. When a Target sins in his thoughts, in his fantasies—in his daily routine!—it's just a matter of time before we station the *actual* sin under his nose and watch him lap it up like a Lhasa Apso. Even if a transgression never actually occurs, bestowal of the "gift" is seriously suppressed by ample amounts of static.

After you've successfully prompted your Target to sin, you will then face the Opposition's second line of defense, namely *guilt*. This is also associated with the "light" of conscience nestled inside every soul, but its designs are considerably more shrewd and deceptive. Its message to your pygmy-minded mongrel is that he must *repent*, confess his crime to the Archenemy (and/or one of His comedic representatives) and internally forsake the sin. Not just for a season, but *forever*.

Now ponder the Archenemy's most demented paradox: No matter how often your Target falls prey to our seductions, no matter how many lassos we loop around his soul—no matter how much energy, time, and resources we invest in his incarceration—all he needs to do is repent, and the Opposition slices all of our fetters, wipes the slate clean, and allows him a new beginning, a fresh go at the game! It's dispiritingly frustrating!

But take heart, my able apprentice. There looms a shimmering silver lining. If we can induce your boy to merely revisit the sin, the way will conspicuously open wide for us to reintroduce all of our cuddly old coils—and add several new nooses to boot!

So therein lies your stratagem, Frogknot. Mr. Hansen must be encouraged to repeat a sin over and over and over again. He must become *addicted* to it. He must be made to believe the breath of life itself might cease to flow through his body without it. Now is when you must bludgeon your Target's self-esteem more viciously than ever. He must see himself as the weakest wretch on the planet—a helpless slave to our irrepressible will.

This is a critical crossroad. Smoke and mirrors become your consummate allies. *Never* allow your Target to conceive a means of escape. You must help him avoid every setting that might offer him the vaguest glimmer of hope that emancipation is even possible. Over time we'll have the elfin rascal so twisted and tormented that he can't bear to face his own mug in the mirror.

However, even after you help him to reach this state of desolation, don't think for an instant that the war is won. Such an attitude of demoralization is not entirely undesirable to the Opposition either. I've known countless imps in my department who will at this juncture turn their backs in a premature moment of self-congratulation and discover, to their shock and dismay, that the Target has fallen to his knees in an awful exhibition of sorrow and shame. The Target will have thrown himself upon the Archenemy's mercy. He may confess, to our mortification, that without such grace, he is entirely lost. It's a sickening scene! What's more, it's exactly what the Archenemy was *hoping* would transpire all along!

Don't you see? He *wants* them to discover and embrace this dependence. Acknowledging such tripe is pivotal to His unscrupulous plan. Quite often this is a moment when our myriads of minions eternally forfeit our firmest grasp. Most agonizing is when it suddenly hits a tempter like yourself that he's been playing *right into the Archenemy's hands!* In such cases we've actually *assisted* Him in achieving His objective! Oh, such a realization is bitterly disconsolating. And not a trifle embarrassing.

No, Frogknot, instead of allowing your Target to succumb to guilt and rush headlong into the Archenemy's embrace, you must reassure him that the only way to eliminate his guilt is by suffocating such emotions *altogether!* He must conclude that guilt itself is incongruous with reason and logic. Help him to extinguish all pangs of conscience. He must begin to view many vices as outside the parameters of sin—distinct and separate from all rational definitions of disobedience. Encourage him to bow to the innermost beast of his defective nature. It's always quite humorous if a Target can be bamboozled into believing that if he fails to surrender to certain sins it may actually be hazardous to his health!

Emphasize the notion that struggling against his inner appetite is a futile and even *arrogant* practice. Urge him to conclude that it was silly to have ever contemplated that he might resist. The truth is, this view is correct. He *can't* conquer us alone. We are far too sneaky and seasoned to be defeated by self-discipline alone. But you must never let him in on this most fervently protected secret. Instead, he must believe it is his incontrovertible lot in life to slay all his dragons without the intervention of heaven. The more you make it a matter of personal pride, the less likely he is to fall to his knees and plead for loftier aid.

To further confound the Archenemy's strategy of using guilt, encourage your boy to judge himself side by side with the standards of the world. That old, arthritic adage—"Everybody else does it, why shouldn't I?"—is never outdated. It's particularly effective if you can expose him to celebrities, sports heroes, medical practitioners, teachers, friends, and even relatives who openly condone and promote specific sins. Advocate settings wherein certain infectious transgressions are merely a running joke, a perpetual punch line. Nothing so monumental as to be taken seriously—so long as the repetition assures him that a particular vice is universal, and that committing such minor infractions is *normal*. Remember the slogan we shouted at all those tedious Institute assemblies?— *"What is normal must become abnormal! What is abnormal must become normal!"* Lastly, you must establish that any person who claims *not* to commit certain sins is flat out lying, or else emotionally and functionally unstable.

So heed my advice, my talented tenderfoot. Until Mr. Hansen's second date with Miss Sessions, flood his thoughts with an endless cavalcade of images and ideas that will inflame his most pernicious fantasies. I trust you won't find your options for ammunition lacking. Start with the game store where he and his classmates gather. The magazine rack at any check-out counter is also at your service. As is the content of his favorite films, internet sites, and countless multimedia resources. Because we've been so successful at suffocating his imagination and stifling his hobbies, he simply cannot escape the veritable avalanche of images. Even the content of everyday advertisements will go a great distance in suggesting privileges and secrets known only to the most beautiful and masculine of the race. Your first victory, Frogknot, is waiting to be plucked. I have every confidence of your inevitable triumph.

But in case you fail, I've enclosed a brochure of our Department's Re-education Camp for Incompetent Tempters, fully illustrated, to emphasize the consequences.

Your Munificent Maestro,
MUCKWHIP

8

From: "Muckwhip" <muckwhip@waydownbelow.hel>
To: <frogknot@waydownbelow.hel>
Subject: unforeseen developments

MY DEAR FROGKNOT,

Spare me your lame litany of excuses. You grovel as if I have no sense of sound judgment or fair play. I assure you, I am teeming with both. I'm perfectly aware that you're not entirely to blame for what has happened. Fortunately for you, I've just finished a hearty brunch consisting of several of your coworkers who've again failed to halt the Organization's progress in yet another African nation. I have therefore no appetite for gristle-ridden rookies such as yourself. I have, however, notified the Re-education Camp of your imminent arrival if you experience any further setbacks, whether it's due to your dereliction or not.

I'm particularly irked to read in your report that "no one could have foreseen" that Mr. Hansen's father would suffer a heart attack the very day before his all-important second date with Miss Sessions. On the contrary, any experienced tempter would have anticipated something like this from a thousand miles off. This is precisely the kind of stunt the Opposition attempts whenever we are within mere centimeters of scoring a resounding victory. It's really Sputcurse—the fiend in charge of his father—who deserves my harshest discipline. Why was I not informed that this man was so close to a physical breakdown? Curse the Opposition! Once again we see that their methods are inexcusably devious and premeditated. Such an event might, if we are not quick to respond, obliterate years of painstaking progress. And don't think for a minute that *I* will be held accountable. No, no. It's *you*, Frogknot—you and Sputcurse and all the other miserable imps in charge of this family—who will pay and pay dearly.

And if any one of you is for one second entertained by this crisis, think again! Yes, yes, I too in the murkily distant past allowed myself to bask in the sheer pleasure of human suffering, to smirk at death, pain, and mourning like a gluttonous fool slobbering over a strip of half-cooked bacon. But know this and know it well: In the end it is virtually *always* a tool of the Archenemy! Never mind the seeming inconsistency. Or did you fail to grasp that He *permits* suffering, pain, and grief to gratify His own self-serving ends? It invariably becomes His secret weapon, His sure-fire prescription for jarring human beings into rethinking their place in the universe. The unhappy result is generally that the Archenemy, His gospel, and His kingdom become more sharply attuned in the Target's daily contemplations.

Never mind. The damage is done. Your job now is to launch an immediate, full-scale offensive against your boy's conception of fairness and veracity. Youth are particularly vulnerable on this point. They'll blast the trumpet of injustice whenever faced with major or even minor tragedies, as well as trifling "inconveniences." The only way to keep Mr. Hansen from turning to the Archenemy is to prompt him to turn *inward*. If your boy can become absorbed in his own misery, repeatedly muttering "Why me?" or "Woe is me!" then and *only* then are we in Hell allowed to relish any pleasure at human suffering.

Sputcurse informs me that the Target's father did, in fact, survive the heart attack and is at present recovering in a nearby hospital. This is regrettable. If he had expired, the man would have been most assuredly ours. As it is, Sputcurse faces the prospect of watching forty years of focused, intensive labor flushed into the sewer. He has no imp to blame but himself. I told him years ago that if he didn't lead the boy's father toward ever deeper indulgences of appetite and addiction, some half-baked calamity like this was bound to occur. Even now this oaf is engaged in rigorous reflection about his life and any lasting contribution he may have made in the temporal realm. Sputcurse will be picking up the pieces for weeks, maybe months.

But don't worry yourself about his impending punishments, my apprentice. Your task remains clear. Don't allow your bettlebug to spend any time pondering the eternal ramifications of such nonsense. This is always an odious road. Instead, urge him to seek refuge *away* from it all. Convince him that he must escape the pressure. Tantalize him with whatever sin you deem best. Despite appearances, this is a *perfect* time to convey him into the clutches of Miss Sessions. Let him envision her embrace as a guaranteed remedy against all earthly anxiety. You might also introduce him to his first taste of narcotics. There are oodles of opportunities. Must I make you a laundry list? Go to! Have at it! Attack!

If you can rope this boy into one vice—one deliciously wicked indulgence—an adorable scene indeed will start to unfold. We see it time and time again in the lives of teenagers brought up in the Organization. Once they get a taste of some delectable sin, they'll often proceed to shatter every edict that ever restrained them. They will declare, in essence, "Well, I messed up once. Might as well mess up *all the way!*"

This is, admittedly, an exquisitely satisfying moment for all of us in the Lower Realms. My own description of such exhilaration could never do it justice. To ensure that it happens, you must contort your Target's definition of *good* and *bad*. Let him deduce that the difference between them is as murky as mud. Once you cross over that line, there's no going back. Advise him he must now wear the badge of being "bad" for all time and don the appropriate trappings. If some meddling Church leader or guardian tries to tell him that righteousness is a *direction* rather than a position, distract his attention with the latest viral video. Or better yet, cloud his thoughts with fear and dread regarding the current crisis with his father.

Your next report had better be brimming over with decisive news of your Target's spiraling descent. Spare me none of the juicier details. In light of other news I'm receiving about the dedication of yet another of the Organization's gaudy temples, I may be in dire need of a few phrases of good cheer.

Your Amicable Administrator,
MUCKWHIP

9

From: "Muckwhip" <muckwhip@waydownbelow.hel>

To: <frogknot@waydownbelow.hel>

Subject: miss paxton

MY DEAR FROGKNOT,

How *dare* you prattle on about an "unexpected turn of events" or "solid hopes for progress in the future!" It's no use trying to gloss over the situation. The long and short of it is that you have let things devolve from bad to worse.

Really, Frogknot, did you actually think that just because his first effort at prayer was a monotonous monologue of inarticulate ramblings that the Archenemy would be unlikely to respond? Have you lost your limited mind? Have you given permanent leave to your perspicacity? Did Professor Foggoblin teach you nothing? Would your years at the Institute have been better spent fashioning spittoons to catch the drool of our Headmaster's gargoyles?

For nearly a decade your boy has been talking to the Archenemy much the same way that a carnival clown talks to his pet cockatiel. Rarely have his supplications consisted of more than twenty or thirty words. Customarily they've only been articulated in church or over some slobbery meal. And *never* have they been spoken without the pell-mell objective of arriving at the end in the briefest possible span. Now the stubby nebbish, seemingly behind your back, has gone and put his whole heart into it! He got down on both knees and *talked* to the Archenemy. Really *talked* to Him. The whole thing was revolting. Forget the fact that much of what he muttered involved fears of the future and a tedious rhapsody on self-doubt. You can be quite certain the words reached their intended destination. *He* was listening! And in reply He showered down such an outpouring of compassion you'd have thought He hadn't heard from the brat in eons. It was like watching some toad-like alien "phoning home" and receiving in reply an armada of mother ships!

Do you see what has happened, Frogknot? Do you comprehend the full impact of this disaster? The termite may actually think he now has a *testimony*. Before long we'll see him standing behind that repulsive podium once per month along with the rest of those pathetic bleaters—the same abysmal pulpit he used to parody under his breath for all its superficiality and pomp.

And don't think I failed to notice how your report conveniently skipped any mention of your Target's misadventures with Miss Sessions. Were you hoping I might overlook it? Are you so naïve as to think that I have only *your* news reports to depend upon? My secret police have kindly updated me on the situation and I am justifiably horrified. Not only has their relationship fizzled into one of innocuous friendship, but because of your Target's professed desire to serve a mission, Miss Sessions is—out of the clear blue— questioning her loyalty to *us!* We now stand to lose not only Mr. Hansen, but the services of one of our most efficient and faithful operatives!

And what about this Miss Traci Paxton that he met at the game store? Don't pretend not to know whom I mean! The girl he met just before he quit the store to work for the delivery service! (Another of your blunders for which you will be held to full account!) Although you deliberately failed to mention her, I am informed that he's become quite chummy with this puritan prissy. As I read this girl's dossier, I retched with disgust. The self-righteous shrew. The Victorian prude. Even though she comes from a broken and financially destitute home, my finest fiends cannot seem to make a significant dent in her defenses. Half the time they can't even get *near* her! The Archenemy's lackeys brood over her like Dobermans. We can't even goad her to envy the wealth of others. It's almost as if she doesn't *know she's poor!* As if she cannot grasp that nearly every dress she owns is practically a hand-me-down from the handcart pioneers! Our best hope of beating her at her own game seems to reside in her compulsion to rescue little lost puppies like your Target. As far as we can tell, she will quickly lose interest as soon as she fails to reach her lofty expectations. But it may be *years* before we can fully exploit this deficiency.

She is a nuisance of the highest order. Her association with Mr. Hansen must be halted at any cost. Just being in her presence should make your boy feel as if all his inadequacies are blazing as brightly as Hong Kong Harbor at New Year's. Advise him that Miss Paxton feels no genuine attachment, but is solely on a mission of mercy. That should be simple enough. After all, it's partly true. Her attraction to him increased tenfold the instant she heard that he was contemplating a mission. If your boy can be made to suspect that Miss Paxton's devotions are as artificial as silicone, you will exploit a rift that will make their relationship unendurable.

If you play this game with just the right subtlety, I'll tell you precisely what will happen. You will foster in him a determined (albeit unconscious) desire to see this prima donna definitively corrupted. He will become obsessed with pulling her down to his own sewage-sodden level. I doubt he will succeed, but the corollary bitterness and the bruises to his fragile ego will ignite a spectacle of ill feeling that you can quickly transform into full-blown enmity. Your boy already has a nasty habit of transferring hatred of self and hatred of others into hatred for the Organization. This is without a doubt your surest course for unraveling his current perceptions. Only with unwavering diligence can you speedily restore that lovely negative attitude that formerly held him bound.

I shouldn't have to tell you, Frogknot, if your Target submits any mission papers, retribution will be swift and certain. This is your final warning. Time is running out. I suggest you redouble your efforts immediately. Despite the fact that our Department is already grossly over budget for the fiscal year, I am extending to you an increase in resources for the purpose of chloroforming your Target's newfound spiritual well-being and darkening his resurging spiritual intellect. You may afflict your boy at will with a gargantuan hailstorm of gloominess and esteem-smashing depression. Let's just see him pray his way out of *this* one!

Your Determined Dementor,
MUCKWHIP

10

From: "Muckwhip" <muckwhip@waydownbelow.hel>

To: <frogknot@waydownbelow.hel>

Subject: glimmering hope

MY DEAR FROGKNOT,

For once your bi-weekly report did *not* inspire spewing and sputtering. Well, perhaps there was a *twinge* of disappointment. My latest cookbook featured a tantalizing recipe that suited you perfectly, slow-baked in a caramelized glaze. Tentatively, I will place it back onto the shelf with the page marked for easy retrieval. Also on my desk is a transfer document awaiting a mere flourish of my pen. Frankly, it's been a bit of a challenge determining whether you are better suited for pain or potluck? No matter. I will postpone my verdict. You see? I am not such a grouchy, iron-fisted administrator after all!

Your exploitation of unfounded rumors surrounding his new crush, Miss Paxton, was magnificently managed. Were you aware that such whispers were initially set in motion by a certain Bradley Railsback, who escorted Miss Paxton to a recent highly-visible social occasion at their high school? Pairing them up for this party was hardly an accident. We'd carefully orchestrated the event for months, confident that such a union would reap sumptuous rewards, no matter the outcome. We felt sure that merely the *association* would pay sizable dividends, as is now proving to be true.

You see, Mr. Railsback represents one of my proudest achievements, especially amongst those whom the Organization might raise up as a lofty standard for other adolescents to exemplify. In his capacity as a priest, we are frequently gratified that his mellifluent voice is employed to utter the sacrament prayer in a manner that makes even widows and 'tweeners swoon. Yet thanks to our occasional encouragements, he is as morally bankrupt as any teen of the modern age. As a certified jock of Cascadia High School, he views himself as Hercules's sole successor and inordinately relishes the sensation of vanquishing and humiliating his fellow beings. The fact that our Cinderella spurned her prince's initial advances, and that their date terminated before arriving at the ball, is beside the point. It was actually *I* who coerced Mr. Railsback, through his halfwit tormentor, Piddlegrim (the *only* imp even assigned since Bradley has proven so malleable), to hatch such vengeful innuendos against Miss Paxton in the first place.

A succulent hearsay remains one of our most effective contrivances for instigating chaos and ill will. It nearly always penetrates otherwise bulletproof scenarios. The key is suffusing the venom through a syndicate of weak-minded sycophants whose egos are nourished by publicizing the blemishes and warts of others. As humankind has no shortage of such vermin, dissemination was surprisingly breezy.

However, since Mr. Railsback does not normally pass through Mr. Hansen's usual orbit, you are to be commended for placing him in the company of Mr. Frederick Tannenbaum, a gossip gold medalist. As you nimbly foresaw, Mr. Tannenbaum willingly regurgitated to Mr. Hansen any and all filth and debauchery that he could describe, thus planting in Mr. Hansen's hormonally elevated hubris the idea that if he failed to reach first base, his image might as well appear under the Wikipedia heading of "invertebrate jellyfish."

So I say "bravo," Frogknot! Your goading and teasing of Mr. Hansen the week prior to his date with Miss Paxton unearthed a treasure trove of opportunities. I was at first concerned that an unfavorable opinion of her might elicit a cancellation of their plans. But as we have repeatedly observed, there is no creature among the Archenemy's creations more predictable in its thought-patterns than an adolescent male.

Yes, his respect for her was compromised just as his imagination was stimulated. Inflated pride did the rest, hatching a sort of quasi-competition between two distant acquaintances—Hansen and Railsback—ensuring the thing your boy attempted. Sure, he trembled in his shoes most of the evening, stuttering much like an animated pig. Nevertheless, the attempt, when it played out, was a stellar performance. Forgive me for deploying operatives with recording devices. Our hope was that excerpts might make the cut on Hell's Wickedest Home Videos. Notification is pending.

In any case, the clumsily-forced kiss, the emphatic shove, the violent slap, and the attendant tears inspired rousing applause from those of us in our box seats. My only concern was that you punched the "shame" accelerator too aggressively. Shame is an emotion that should be strategically delayed. In reality, it serves us only if it morphs into hatred—hatred of Miss Paxton, yes!—but preferably against the entire female species. Better yet, hatred for humanity! Bellwether cynicism and black despondency are your ultimate goals. If shame arises too readily, it transforms into remorse, and remorse into repentance. This can unwittingly turn a stunning victory into abject failure.

But never mind. Watching as your Target damaged his pickup truck while consumed in frustration, obliterating his neighbor's brick mailbox, was an unanticipated encore. The neighbor's profanity?—eloquent! His father's coarse replies?—equally superb! I started to wonder if another heart attack might be in the works, but oh well.

Let me add that the most gratifying reaction was his mother's merciless silence. This may have assured your boy's terminal self-loathing more than Miss Paxton's rejection. Just wait for the bill from the body shop and brick mason! Therein materializes the most practical consequence of our success. My analysts tell me that his oh-so-precious truck will have to be sold to satisfy the debt.

As once voiced in your Target's chambers of government, "No good crisis should ever go to waste." It is now in your grasp to capitalize on these events in a most capital way. The veritable idea of a mission will certainly be dismissed. Moreover, Mr. Hansen will become a piñata of ridicule not only amongst his peers, but his church-going neighbors. I'll have a few dependable tempters plant in the minds of his ward's more influential gossips that narcotics are to blame for the accident, not inflamed temper. This is more believable anyway. The scuttlebutt will spread like wildfire. His bishop will certainly slam the books on his futile efforts to inspire Mr. Hansen to enlist as an Organizational ambassador.

Keep stoking the flames, dear Frogknot! Affix the stamp of humiliation with rivets. I anticipate that your next report will contain the most encouraging reading to date. Oh, but I do know talent when I see it! YOU, my esteemed fiend, are destined for greatness!

Your Jubilant General,
MUCKWHIP

11

From: "Muckwhip" <muckwhip@waydownbelow.hel>
To: <frogknot@waydownbelow.hel>
Subject: travel arrangements

MY DEAR, DEAR FROGKNOT,

Enclosed you will find all the necessary papers for your immediate transfer to our most infamous Reeducation Camp for Incompetent Tempters. I have personally gone to the trouble to furnish your quarters with all the latest and greatest devices of disfigurement and torture. We hope that your stay will be memorable. To assist in your travel arrangements, I've dispatched two of my most reliable henchmen. Don't let their appearance startle you. So many spiked, flaming protrusions may indeed be excessive, but you should be far more terrified by the thought of how they will treat you en route. I've put them under no obligation to show the least restraint.

I hardly think an explanation is warranted. You knew this was coming. Your Target, having successfully submitted his papers for a mission, and having received his call to some swamp-infested dungheap in the southern United States, is now ready to embark upon an exclusive two-year escapade in the Archenemy's service. The howls of anguish still echo through the columns and catacombs of Hell.

How could you have let this happen? We *knew* this boy! We *all* knew him! He was there at the very beginning, driving his shafts and thorns into our sides as far back as the War in Heaven. His dossier should have offered to you an emblazoned reminder of his foreordained potential. At the same time, it should have highlighted all of his most glaring deficiencies. It's clear now that you failed to capitalize upon a single one.

Don't try to earn my sympathies with drivel about how his recent conflict with Miss Paxton produced the opposite effect. I'm perfectly aware of how she succored the boy's wounded ego in an appalling display of *deus ex machina,* forgiving him outright and establishing a genuine friendship—even promising to correspond throughout his southern states deployment! Moreover, I will listen to no further babblings about how the Archenemy's Spirit kept you at bay more effectively with each passing day. If you'd followed my advice from the outset, you'd have never had to grapple with that terrible Presence in the first place!

Now look at the result! Our accountants are still trying to assess the damage. Fresh deficits are added almost hourly. If you happen to hear screaming in the cell next to your own, it will be the wails of your pea-brained compatriot, Sputcurse. As you no doubt noticed amidst the chaos, the boy's father attended his farewell address! Not only this, but the man has recommitted to full activity in the Organization during his son's absence. Well . . . we'll just see about that.

It is my fondest wish, Frogknot, that you will not look upon your incarceration as punishment, but rather as an opportunity for "re-enlightenment." This is an invaluable opportunity to hone your skills as a tempter while my lesser minions are simultaneously sharpening your septum upon a grindstone.

As far as the young Mr. Stuart Hansen is concerned, you needn't concern yourself with his *un*well-being. A number of replacement tempters are already being interviewed. If your re-education proves successful—and I'm sure that it will—you will be joining them upon your undetermined date of release. In the meantime I have made it my personal mission to precipitate this young man's downfall. Mark my words, Frogknot! Stuart will one day become stew or I am not our infernal father's Supernal Viceroy of Vice, Muckwhip the Unmerciful, M.B.A., ThD., XXL., Esq. etc., etc.!

Your Unassuming Overlord,
MUCKWHIP

Part II:

AGAINST MISSIONARIES

12

From: "Muckwhip" <muckwhip@waydownbelow.hel>

To: <frogknot@waydownbelow.hel>

Subject: welcome back!

MY DEAR FROGKNOT,

Allow me to be the very first to hail your return to the happy services of our infernal father. I understand that your reeducation was a rousing success. Didn't I tell you? A little depravation, disembowelment, and paroxysmal agony never hurt anyone. And in your case I understand it did a *world* of good. I am told there never was a pit viper, wounded wolverine, or rabid Rottweiler more vicious than you in your current state. Oh, Frogknot, I am so proud! I feel like a parent at graduation.

Now that it's over, can you admit to me your immeasurable debt of thanks? Of course you can. You will assuredly gush with gratitude upon your arrival for the benefit of all other tempters in my employ. If you don't feel up to this, then perhaps your internment ended too soon. And for Hell's sake don't worry yourself about any lingering PTSD. Cold sweats, trembling, and random fits of screaming will diminish over time.

Think how much more prepared you are for your present assignment! No level of maliciousness could ever over-qualify you for what's ahead. Young *Elder* Hansen (such a pretentious title!), having regrettably completed his missionary training, has just been assigned his first area to proselytize. Unlike your earlier assignment where this Target's destruction was predominantly placed in your care, you are now part of an elite *squadron* of imps. Every member of your unit has been assigned an identical mission—to sandblast this young miscreant into a mound of dust and chaff that might be dispersed by the wind over multiple acres! You are now part of an illustrious brain trust, a proven think tank, an exclusive committee, and a veritable Seal Team 6 of mayhem and subjugation. Only the most experienced and talented tempters in my department are serving at your sides.

Surely you're aware, no species of mortal is more despised by our infernal father than a full-time missionary. So even if we remain soberly optimistic that Elder Hansen's prospects for success are embarrassingly low, we are nonetheless taking no chances. You will find at your disposal every weapon of temptation ever conceived. Nothing less than our most advanced, top-of-the-line technologies.

You might be wondering why so many co-tempters have been allocated to someone as paltry and insignificant as Elder Stuart Hansen. I assure you it's not because we're *afraid* of missionaries. Perish the thought! These feeble-minded snivelers are still the same lanky, immature, gas-passing troglodytes they always were. It's because we *are* afraid of—no, no, I will not use that word. It's because we are *mildly concerned* about *Him*— that is to say, the Archenemy—and all of the resources He brings to bear to defend and protect these ill-prepared grunts.

The sheer volume of the Archenemy's assets is astonishing, Frogknot. We have yet to discover where He acquires such resources. We've studied His accounts time and again and feel certain that His supplies are very nearly exhausted. They *must* be! Any other conclusion is a mathematical impossibility!

Nevertheless, He throws all discretion and sound business acumen to the wind and provides for His missionaries an inexhaustible supply of cutting-edge, state-of-the-art weaponry.

Yes, I know. It makes no practical sense. These are 18-year-old boys, for Hell's sake! Can you think of any policy more deranged, any strategy more unsound, any curriculum more cockeyed than to entrust an entire corporation's advance and progress to 18- and 19-year-old boys? At no other period of a male's lifespan is he more brimming over with selfishness, pride, inconsistency, and hormones than he is at 18. Might as well toss foxes into chicken coops, assign flame-throwers to children, or seat blind men in the cockpits of 747s!

Of course if *we* had been put in charge of the situation (as was humbly suggested by our infernal father from the very beginning) only the most seasoned, educated, and experienced members would have been allowed to proselytize. What am I saying?? If *we'd* been at the helm, missionary work would have been wholly *unnecessary!* Skeptics would have been jolted with cattle prods at the first sign of disobedience. Unfortunately, the Opposition has never grasped such an enlightened approach.

The arsenal of defenses available to these mere toddlers is downright dizzying. Never was a thicker fog, a deeper quagmire, or a more formidable obstacle course set in place for our forces to infiltrate. However, despite this disparity, our tactics have not changed. The question remains: Does the proselytizer *utilize* these defenses? And in the case of Elder Hansen, herein lies our best advantage! It is the perpetual chink in his armor. Never forget, your Target is no less answerable to the effects of sin. In certain respects, he's even *more* vulnerable. Let me explain.

Possibly during no other time in mortality will Mr. Hansen be more accountable for his actions than during this two-year charade. He now contends with a multitude of additional rules that he has never before faced. There are rules regarding practically everything: waking up, going to bed, preparation, companionship, entertainment, travel, expenditures . . . the list goes on! In essence, by agreeing to serve a mission, your Target has strapped a ball and chain to his ankle that will restrict his behavior in every aspect of his life. Why *any* person—least of all a self-absorbed 18-year-old—would *voluntarily* submit to such enslavement is beyond us. However, this is also their Achilles heel. For the next 24 months, every breach of these seemingly trivial rules is now classified as *sin*. Who'd have thought that diving into a swimming pool could be sinful? But it *is*, Frogknot! I know it sounds preposterous, but if you can incline a missionary to hit the snooze button on his alarm, you will suddenly find yourself granted greater access to tempt him, greater power to bind his soul. Don't laugh. This stuff is deadly serious.

Your principal challenge is to suppress any reminders about how obedience leads to increased opportunities, strengths, defenses, etc. I'm always surprised how quickly the natural advantages of obedience are forgotten by the snivelers. But *especially* while serving a mission, when one is so engulfed in the heat of battle!

I discern that Elder Hansen is now particularly susceptible. He is just now starting to wonder what in the name of Ninevah he has gotten himself into? And so it is time to strike. Only a marginal effort will be required to pressure him to the point where he believes he is literally *suffocating*. Every day he is increasingly inclined to self-combust with regret over this lunatic choice, all the freedoms he has jettisoned, and the misery he has self-inflicted. Remind him that it's never too late to see the so-called light. The world he knew still awaits him, more appealing than he even remembers. You may even hit the jackpot. Think of it! You may compel him to *go home*. Imagine the all-out celebration, the gratuitous promotions, and the resplendent rewards that await you and your comrades were you to tally such a victory! Whole careers are made from this kind of success, Frogknot. In one fell swoop you could find yourself a Tempter First Class! Visualize it. Relish it. And lick your lips at the savory feasts that await.

Now go and get 'em, my prized pit bull! Remember your experience in the re-education camp as you reflect upon your new golden rule: *Do unto your Target as your torturers and tormentors did unto you!* Your comrades are eager to brief you on moment-to-moment developments.

You're Admirable Admiral,
MUCKWHIP

13

From: "Muckwhip" <muckwhip@waydownbelow.hel>

To: <frogknot@waydownbelow.hel>

Subject: bureaucracy

MY DEAR FROGKNOT

It is my privilege to report that each of your comrades have texted urgent dispatches calling for your ouster. They describe you as a "pugnacious, hackneyed, blatherskite with the intelligence of an endomorph." You should consider this highly flattering. Had I heard otherwise, I might have wavered in my conviction at having assembled the most carnivorous team of tempters in my long career. If you're pondering the whereabouts of your colleague, Nitwibble, you should know that he was your only co-worker who labeled you "an able tempter of indefatigable potential." I forthwith transferred him to Outer Mongolia to work alongside a bike-pedaling elder from Duckwater, Nevada. Such are my rewards for impotent niceties. Only the most rapacious imps are to be exalted in this department. Such character is essential to achieve the objective at hand.

Am I to understand that your eager-beaver Target, Elder Hansen, has been delayed in his desire to start door-knocking on day one of his adventure? Ah, bureaucracy can be a beautiful thing! These boll weevils spend weeks prepping for that first discussion with the ostensible golden contact only to discover that life still moves at the speed of . . . *life!* Let this be the first of *many* occasions where pledged presumptions fail to reach actual expectations.

I'm pleased that he must begin his assignment with a two-or-three day furlough to secure new digs. What? Is it possible that he does not perceive this as a furlough? See that he *does*, Frogknot! Few missionaries can maintain a sadistic 6-day/16-hour regimen of uninterrupted proselytizing. And you certainly cannot allow such habits to become ingrained. Longer and longer respites that emphasize the cares and comforts of the world must routinely disrupt such patterns. Rarely will a full-time elder combine laundry and lecturing, shopping and sermonizing. And neither should his radar be activated to seek investigators while house-hunting.

As you have undoubtedly gleaned for yourself, such intermissions from missionary work are frequently sought by his trainer, Elder Winthorpe. When the mission president combined these two diametrical personalities, I knew that we were in for a treat. Elder Hansen had for months envisioned a missionary mentor more superhero than human, an amalgamation of Captain America, Bruce Banner, and Bruce R. McConkie. Instead he is yoked with a thin wisp of a wimp who shudders at the twitch of his own shadow.

From the starting gate your Target was required to grab the reins of leadership and adopt the role of alpha-dog to a cowering cockapoo. We have often chuckled at Winthorpe's insipid door approaches and graceless "golden questioning"— sometimes with such revelry that I'm astonished our laughter did not penetrate his eardrums along with his subconscious. Our only concern is that Winthorpe's humility somewhat exceeds his homeliness. In time this could admittedly prove irksome. Humility seems to garner an abundance of brownie points from the Opposition that can eventually disrupt a tempter's perfectly executed offense.

But enough about Winthorpe. He's not your main concern. Elder Hansen accepted helmsmanship of the twosome as surely as Rommel accepted command of the 7th Panzers. But make note—it was accompanied by a subtle chord of resentment. So there's your angle, Frogknot. As I am oft inclined to quote: "Pride prowleth before the plunge." Again your Target's ego is the thing. As frequently as you can cajole Elder Hansen into belittling, patronizing, and demolishing Elder Winthorpe's self-esteem, the greater our eventual rewards. If we cannot presently hurt your Target, let your Target pound his companion into complete apathy and submission. Your elder avoided such pencil-pushers in his regular life. Let him cringe at the prospect of having no other daily conversation except with this spindly, introverted geek who is as helpless as a stalk of chard without his security blankets of handheld electronics. The fiends in charge of Elder Winthorpe are under strict orders to frazzle their subject's nerves. Thus, you must prick Elder Hansen's gargantuan lack of patience. Not a difficult exercise, as you already know.

As for their current exploits locating a new domicile, can you spin a bit of mathematical magic? Can you stretch two days into ten? Can you convince them that comfort must outweigh functionality? I suppose it's of no use to emphasize the presence of swimming facilities, but what about tennis courts, saunas, exercise rooms, etc.? Yes, I understand their budgetary limitations. But do *they?* Your Target does not seem to have wrapped his head around such restrictions. Continue to distract and bemuse.

Penury should have no place in your elder's perception of mission life. As he churns his memories of home, you must highlight every former convenience. This will encourage him at each potential apartment to question the firmness of the mattress, size of the closet, quality of air conditioning, and texture of the toilet lid. Every domicile must be declared unsuitable according to any of a thousand rationales. As their search drags on, the clock tick-tocks, the sun rises and sets, and countless souls remain enslaved to our infernal father's will.

Be assured, chop-chop *will* lead to chomp-chomp, so long as you remain vigilant and undaunted. Additional arsenal will be deployed as needed. Keep your weaponry sharp, polished, and close at hand. Long before this exploit is concluded, you will become adept at wielding each and every implement of anguish.

I'm informed that as soon as your duo finally settles upon a new dwelling, Elder Winthorpe will introduce Elder Hansen to his first genuine investigator. Oh, the frolics that await you! I must confess a slight twinge of jealousy. This is when the fun *really* begins!

Your Gleeful Governor,
Muckwhip

14

From: "Muckwhip" <muckwhip@waydownbelow.hel>

To: <frogknot@waydownbelow.hel>

Subject: investigator

MY DEAR FROGKNOT,

Let me remind you that your assignment is Elder Hansen, *not* his investigator, Mr. Moody. We have the situation well in hand with regard to this dysfunctional amoeba. At first you might suppose that Mr. Moody's downfall is not our department's concern. Think again. It is and has always been the longstanding policy of our infernal father that as soon as any soul takes an active interest in the Organization we are instantly allowed, as a matter of inter-office protocol, unrestrained access to an investigator's records. It's a remarkable thing to behold. At no time is the level of camaraderie between departments more harmonious—a glowing tribute to a longstanding tradition of *espirit de corps* in the Lower Realms. Besides, if any tempters in charge of Mr. Moody *failed* to co-operate, I'd have full authority to deliver them up to the sausage makers.

Be aware, the imps who have charge of Mr. Moody are fully reinforced. Not that any special attention is required. You see, Mr. Moody is what is commonly referred to as a "professional" investigator. This means that he has already invited the missionaries into his home on countless occasions, joyfully wasting humongous chunks of their schedule, asking a thousand senseless questions—and all on the premise that he is sincerely interested in learning the truth. In reality, he just enjoys the elders' attention. He relishes their bouts of sparring and repartee.

In Mr. Moody's world, he's hopelessly stuck in a dissatisfying job, monotonous marriage, and failed family. To our credit, his teenage offspring have all grown irretrievably distant. He considers the missionaries an amusing distraction in his otherwise humdrum day. It also gives him an opportunity to exercise his cerebral wits. Oh, how we love lovers of knowledge who lack knowledge of love!

If you haven't noticed, his wife of 21 years has yet to join him in these discussions. She is far too engrossed in her own private hobbies. She paints tigers, if you can believe it. Obsessed with the orange-striped felines. Their home is littered with dozens of oils-on-canvas of tigers—a theme she no doubt adopted in hopes that her husband might someday *become* one, generate a predator's spine, and perhaps a few throat-slashing claws, in order to improve his prospects at providing her with a more luxuriant life.

Here is where considerable progress can be made regarding Elder Hansen's overall effectiveness as a missionary. Our bombardment is specifically directed at your Target's so-called "testimony." Right now this testimony is as fragile as a skyscraper of playing cards. It's never been challenged intellectually. All his life he's been nestled in the security of his predominantly Mormon community. As a result, he is over-confident—even cocky—about his theological prowess. No soul has ever challenged him to an all-out mud-slinging duel centered on our favorite doctrinal disputes.

Remind me sometime and I'll send over some hilarious footage of Mr. Moody's previous encounters with unprepared elders. Some missionaries have left his presence visibly shaken. One broke down in tears as he tried to reconcile the host of "politically incorrect" tenets ingrained in the Organization's belief system. Of late this angle has produced a particularly bounteous harvest. All we have to do is define the Archenemy's edicts as offensive or unseemly, and we can often induce outright apostasy. A target's alternative is facing a veritable phalanx of "political correctness" police who are prepared to bludgeon all believers into total passivity. Very few have the courage to resist.

Yes, pure apostasy is a sweet reward, but it is not necessarily your goal at this juncture. Instead, you must neutralize whatever passion or conviction your Target harbors toward the very cause he represents. Great care must be taken with this approach. Our strategy can easily backfire, especially if your Target addresses our apparent checklist of contradictions by seeking insight directly from the Archenemy—while on his *knees!*

To prevent this abomination from taking place, you must strike a decisive blow against Elder Hansen's morale. Plaguing a target with depression, darkness, and despondency will generally thwart him from seeking a spiritual recharge from loftier realms. Work very closely with your compatriots to ensure the proper execution of tactics and timing. Otherwise, Mr. Hansen's convictions could become more ingrained than we could have imagined. His testimony might inflate to where your ability to confuse and demoralize is utterly crushed. The worst case scenario would be to discover that your Target is laying all questions and doubts at the feet of the Archenemy as a matter of *routine.* He could even reach the point that he no longer *needs* intellectual solutions to our most delicious controversies—because his *faith* in the Opposition is overriding! A nauseating predicament, to say the least.

Just keep your Target desperately searching for solutions to Mr. Moody's myriad of "concerns." This is where Elder

Hansen's pride should serve you well. If there's anything this blustering imbecile despises, it's losing an argument. Mark my words. The boy will fight to the death before conceding defeat. Rest assured that your comrades in other departments will provide Mr. Moody with countless questions to keep your Target and his companion engrossed. Over the years we've supplied this investigator with a list of disputations long enough to cross the eyes of even the most erudite elders.

Again, what we're really burning through is *time,* Frogknot. Just as with house-hunting and other distractions, our purpose is to misemploy gross amounts of precious minutes, hours, and days that might otherwise be applied seeking prospects more vulnerable to the missionaries' message.

In this case we make headway on multiple levels: masticating time, undermining testimony, and promoting anti-Organizational propaganda. I expect to see detailed progress reports with regard to each. And don't think that you can attempt any of the juvenile shenanigans you played before your re-education. Glossing over pertinent information or omitting details that you think will posture your efforts in a more positive light will not be tolerated. Remember, I receive similar reports from every fiend assigned to Elder Hansen, and you know quite well how we deal with backstabbers and Benedict Arnolds in this department. We reward them quite handsomely.

Your Omnipresent Overlord,
MUCKWHIP

15

From: "Muckwhip" <muckwhip@waydownbelow.hel>
To: <frogknot@waydownbelow.hel>
Subject: homesick

MY DEAR FROGKNOT,

So your boy is homesick and misses his female pen pal, Miss Paxton. Oh, *boo hoo! Sniffle, whimper, retch, and hurl!* Serves him right, the groveling lilliputian parasite.

Apparently he didn't realize how much *work* a mission was going to be. Thought the Archenemy's Spirit would do all the work for him, did he? So typical. I've lost count of the number of proselytizers who launch into this farce thinking the instant they are set apart they'll experience glowing, tingling, twinkletoe sensations from their so-called "Holy Ghost" around the clock, their minds so brimming over with hourly revelations that they'll never have a moment's doubt about the most lamebrain decisions. Actually our job is to *encourage* this expectation so that the reality is all the more disenchanting. Still, it never ceases to amaze me how whole-heartedly they fall for it.

Ah, well, all I can say, Frogknot, is *"enjoy!"* These are unequivocally the most satisfying moments of your current assignment. Keep grinding, grinding, grinding him down. Don't let up for an instant. This is your best opportunity to sour his entire attitude. A mission is nothing like what he expected, eh? So drive this point home again and again. Capitalize upon the ignorance, immaturity, and pettiness of other missionaries, especially his newest companion, Elder Lefler. Whisper to your target's mind that these 18 and 19-year-old adolescents are not so different from the clowns and buffoons he hung around with in high school. What, no halos? You mean they still think worldly thoughts? Some are actually *lazy? Obnoxious?* Downright *devilish?* (No compliment intended.) Allow him to focus only upon these aspects of their characters, Frogknot. Affix the proper blinders so that their flaws are the only attributes that he sees.

I like the way you played upon his feelings of "righteous indignation" when his district leader couldn't keep a straight face during morning prayers. And his offense when his new companion sang the questionable lyrics of a catchy pop tune as it blared over the intercom at Pizza Hut. These are all critical notes in his symphony of self-combustion, and enough of them together might lead your elder to wonder what difference it makes whether he completes his mission or not. He might decide he could just as easily serve the Archenemy back home, and simultaneously sleep in a bed where his flesh is not a buffet for bedbugs. He could still attend midnight movie premiers and date his girlfriend.

Even if the awful guilt associated with ultimate failure proves too difficult to swallow and he simply cannot call it quits, you can still render him useless as a servant of the Archenemy, and even—in the sweetest cases—a proverbial wrench in the machinery of *other* missionaries. Remember, it only takes one rotten elder to ruin a companionship—like killing two birds with one stone. His antics might even hamper the entire district, disrupt the zone, and ultimately— if properly publicized—aggravate the Opposition's efforts in that whole region of the country.

I enjoyed reading in your report that the respect he once felt for his mission president is dramatically waning. Missionaries often put their commandant on a "prophet-like" pedestal when they first arrive. The sooner we can pop this bubble, the better. Occasionally the president's own human failings will aid us, but one of the most effective ways of undermining respect for their "fearless leader" is—once again—the ol' rumor mill. There are few microcosms of society that compare to a Mormon mission. Its boundaries may spread across a million square miles, yet it remains a kind of universe unto itself. Everyone manages to keep tabs on everyone else.

Since a companionship is really its own isolated unit, with sometimes limited contact even with other missionaries, it becomes an ideal Petri dish for breeding and expanding every bit of hearsay until it becomes a carcinogenic infirmity. It takes no time whatsoever for a juicy rumor to reach the ears of every elder in the mission. And each version improves with the retelling. A successful mission, in our eyes, is one that teems with misinformation. Such backbiting is especially lovely when directed against the all-powerful mission president.

Pinpoint any missionary who feels his president has treated him unfairly. This isn't difficult. Every mission has a few. And they're generally quite vocal. Rarely will any elder adhere to "Thumper's rule" about saying "nothing at all." So plop your boy in the path of such disgruntled missionaries as often as possible. I know, for instance, that his zone leader feels he should have been advanced to assistant long ago. On several occasions he's hinted that the president plays favorites. This is an excellent start. But there's so much more. We have one elder who's convinced the president runs his regiment like the Nazi S.S. Introduce your Target to this rabble rouser pronto!

Undermining the shepherd's authority in the eyes of his sheep invariably has a debilitating effect upon overall morale. It can cripple a mission for months—even years. I've seen its effects linger long after an elder returns home, sometimes driving a young man out of the Organization for good.

So take full advantage of the mission grapevine. Moreover, I expect your Target to become an enthusiastic participant in disseminating every stitch of dirty laundry. His tendency to harbor grudges makes him a natural. And now that he's pining about home and girlfriends and a lack of variety in his life, his ears should be particularly keen to all negativity.

But heed my stern warning, Frogknot: the surest way to dispel our darkest cloud of negativity is the *work itself!* Some missionaries become so lost in it, so *consumed* by it, that none of our smear campaigns, attacks on self-esteem, or reminders of home have the least effect. Idleness remains our infernal father's favorite workshop. Has your Target noticed that his neighbor in the apartment complex is an accomplished guitar player? Bring him and his companion home early enough one Saturday evening to hear the strumming through his bedroom wall. If anything evokes his sentiments of jealousy and regret about signing up for this two-year debacle, *this* will.

Or perhaps I speak too soon. I've just received some very interesting news. Apparently his faithful *Dulcinea*, Miss Paxton, has just acquired a new suitor—a very ambitious one at that. Your Target doesn't yet know. I am chomping at the bit to observe his reaction when he finally hears. Ooo, the suspense! This could turn out to be exactly the proverbial straw we were seeking.

Your Sniggering Supervisor,
MUCKWHIP

16

From: "Muckwhip" <muckwhip@waydownbelow.hel>
To: <frogknot@waydownbelow.hel>
Subject: WHAT HAPPENED?!

MY DEAR FROGKNOT,

What in Gehenna is going on over there? I'm getting conflicting reports on every front. What do you *mean* you were suddenly and unexpectedly driven out of the home of his investigator, Mr. Moody? I want answers *immediately!* I just received a fax telling me that there are "injuries" in our ranks! INJURIES?? Is this a practical joke? *Who* is injured? What is the extent of the damage? I can't believe what I'm hearing. THIS IS AN OUTRAGE!

The last I was informed, Mr. Moody was set to regale Elder Hansen and his companion, Elder Lefler, with an amusing array of doctrinal poppycock—everything from Adam-God theories to Salamander letters. This should have squandered the entire evening! WHAT IN THE BOWELS OF BABYLON WENT WRONG?

Yes, yes, I realize the Opposition's forces launched some sort of attack. But on what *grounds?* What was their justification? The Archenemy's Spirit has never been present in these discussions before. The only way it could have been

there is if both parties—missionaries and investigator—
invited it in! This implies that there was sincerity, humility,
and an honest desire on the part of all involved to actually
listen to one another. I adamantly refuse to believe it. Mr.
Moody serves *us!* What chord could have possibly been
struck to change these dynamics? I certainly hope it wasn't
your Target who initiated this disaster. Better hope it was the
imps in charge of his companion, because *somebody* is going
to pay HELL!

I will not, *cannot* rest until this matter is resolved. (Not
that I've rested before. I realize for us rest is strictly
forbidden. It's just a figure of speech!) I do have one report—
let me see, where is it? . . . Ah, here! I have a report which
states that Mr. Moody's wife asked him for a divorce this
morning. But this shouldn't have affected things much. She
blathers this threat every few months like clockwork. The
only hint of an explanation I have is from your fellow
tempter, Grungebite, who reports that just before the
Opposition's attack, *your* Target challenged Mr. Moody to
pray. This had better be a typo, Frogknot. Wasn't it *your*
responsibility to permanently deaden Elder Hansen's
confidence in formal supplication? How could he have
challenged his investigator to pray with any snippet of
sincerity unless he felt that his *own* prayers were being heard?
Explain this conundrum *immediately!* Wasn't it you who
reassured me that Elder Hansen's "knee-time" had withered
away to practically nothing? That all he ever prayed about
was his girlfriend and circumstances back home? Was this
another of your insubordinate *exaggerations?!*

No, don't answer that, Frogknot. I doubt it would bode
well for you. There's only one way to soften my rage. That's
if you *get back inside that house! You* lead the assault, you
whining, spluttering whelp! I don't care if every last one of
you imps ends up bruised, battered, and bleeding. Mr.

Moody's next appointment is Tuesday, correct? That means some development in our favor had better transpire between now and then.

I powerfully suggest that you resort to the simplest means of inhibiting the Archenemy's Spirit. Namely, companionship disharmony. Elder Hansen and Elder Lefler are getting along far too well, and yet there are countless ways to start those incisors a-gnashing. One is from Utah. The other is from Idaho. Isn't there enough material in those facts alone? One snores while the other is an insomniac. One keeps his things organized while the other's belongings are strewn across the apartment. The opportunities for conflict are legion! These two should be at each other's throats! Why haven't these tactics been exploited before now?

In the meantime I've filed a request that all tempters in charge of Mr. Moody be promptly lashed at the rack. This situation has now been relegated entirely to *my* department. Additional recruits will be assigned to Mr. Moody's household to assess the damage and configure our counterattack.

But before you think I'm finished with *you*, Frogknot, let me just say that I've caught wind of yet *another* disturbing development. What's this I hear about Elders Hansen and Lefler teaching discussions to their nitwit neighbor, the guitar player? Are you a total frothing fool? I asked you to torture Elder Hansen with this man's strumming through the bedroom wall—not to *introduce* them! How could you be so incomprehensibly sloppy! Didn't you realize their common interests in music would give your Target the most convenient lead-in a missionary could ever hope for? How could you have allowed them to interact? Do you even read my h-mails? Are they labeled as spam? I'm told they talked for hours, establishing a bond of trust that eased as naturally into a discussion of eternal principals as a slug sliding into its shell. It *makes me sick!* I'm *disgusted!* I retch in Technicolor just contemplating it!

I've never been so livid with you, Frogknot! My eyes are crossed with contempt! It now appears that your re-education accomplished exactly *nothing!* Were you under the impression that you had experienced the worst that I can possibly inflict? Don't count on it, amigo. The worst is yet to come if I don't see this supercilious snotwiper of yours cut to ribbons. Now, get off your fleshless derrière and *do something!* I expect hourly reports on both situations—fully footnoted with extensive bibliographies!

Now if you'll excuse me, I have an appointment with my cosmetologist. Apparently while writing this h-mail I turned such a vomitous shade of purple that the discoloration appears permanent and may require corrective surgery.

Your Disconsolate Director,
MUCKWHIP

17

From: "Muckwhip" <muckwhip@waydownbelow.hel>

To: <frogknot@waydownbelow.hel>

Subject: stomach rumblings

MY DEAR FROGKNOT,

Disaster averted! Silence the alarms! Crank back the dial from Defcon 4 to Defcon 3! Nuclear annihilation is no longer imminent, at least as it pertains to Elder Hansen's current investigator. We are firmly back in the saddle. Of course, this is no thanks to *you*, Frogknot, or any of the inept imps in your platoon. All credit belongs to those fine fiends who have charge of Mr. Moody. Their swift response saved the day. Nevertheless, punishments are still pending for you and your compatriots— just as soon as the first fortuity presents itself and your team can be relieved. For now, I am constrained to keep you on the front line, despite my profound preferences otherwise.

It was a grim day indeed when Mr. Moody uttered his first formal prayer. But thanks to my tireless leadership, all prospects for reversal are secure. The devils assigned to this profligate have managed to fog and blur all memory of the so-called "feeling" that was present during his previous encounter with the elders. According to our plan, he is starting to interpret the entire episode as an overemotional response to his present family crisis.

Moody's tempters have corkscrewed him six ways from Sunday, enticing him to think he must have been bamboozled by his own flustered state of mind. He is now considering the possibility that he was charmed by the missionaries' wiles. He leans toward interpreting it all as rumblings in his stomach—a bit of underdone potato, so to speak—rather than a penetration of his heart. Why, he has even considered that his burning in the bosom may have been inspired by our infernal father! I'm totally serious! Can you appreciate the irony?

Unlike you and your fellow flunkies, Mr. Moody's devils are to be highly commended, rewarded, applauded, and promoted. I have obtained for each of them First Class accommodations on the maiden voyage of our luxury cruise liner on the River Styx, complete with marsh view balconies and adjustable lounge chairs. All will be enjoyed while chomping on butter-roasted sinners as they bask in full view of countless thousands of wrathful and sullen souls, floundering helplessly in the mud. Now *that's* a holiday! And it is *theirs*, Frogknot! Not yours! Their vacation begins as soon as our ship departs dry dock—an event anticipated at or around the close of the next millennium.

So how is it that Mr. Moody's tempters achieved such rhapsodic success? Child's play, Frogknot. Mere child's play, along with a pinch of participation from yours truly. Within *hours* after Elder Hansen and his companion had concluded their prayer vigil, our forces were swarming around their investigator like yellow jackets. Over a period of days we'd coaxed back every one of his intellectual arguments, even adding a few additional quandaries. On top of that, his emotional gyrations so befuddled his temperament that we were within mere *inches* of convincing him to rekindle his love affair with Irish malt whiskey—an addiction he felt he'd licked almost a decade ago. *Oh contraire, mon frère!* Soon Mr. Moody will reap the whirlwind, redefining his life as the empty husk that indeed it is. With any luck, he'll blame the Organization and it's emissaries for bringing about such a piquant awareness.

Thus, Frogknot, your failures have, for the time being, been averted. So don't be too dour about it. *Learn* from your mistakes! Realize that we are never so lackadaisical as to ignore a budding testimony or chop off any religious revival at the knees. We strike with a relentless barrage of jabs and feints, thrusts and uppercuts. It doesn't seem to matter how emphatically the investigator is warned of our impending onslaught. They float through their day blithely ill-prepared, often dismissive of the approaching blitzkrieg. Admittedly, the Opposition's arsenal of defenses can be intimidating, but they are rarely exercised to their fullest potential. Neophytes like Mr. Moody do not understand how to wield them. And messengers like Elder Hansen do not grasp the urgency of instruction! So our pact is this: we will keep the investigator from falling to his knees so long as you keep your Target decidedly off his game. Mr. Moody already feels silly about reciting an actual prayer—*aloud* for criminy's sake! We reemphasize this awkward, embarrassing memory promptly at the top of every hour.

And I've just been informed that Elder Hansen and his compatriot plan to starve themselves for their investigator's sake. Such a clichéd response. Fully anticipated. So let us discuss this peculiar practice—and in a fashion much more insightful than what might have been presented in the Institute's syllabus. You see, in the *real* world—that is, in your Target's former civilian reality—the strategy was to help him avoid fasting altogether. But because this aggravating tradition is so entrenched among missionaries, our *modus operandi* has had to adjust to tactics considerably more cunning. The object is to render a fast ineffectual.

This is most often accomplished by obscuring the focus. You see, the nuisance of fasting lies nestled in the infrastructure of the act itself. For some inconceivable reason, the Archenemy has a steadfast policy of rewarding those who sacrifice something—*anything*—in order to achieve some presupposed "greater good." Don't attempt to comprehend the logic. The effort is certain to short-circuit your brain's fragile synapses. Our most astute researchers conclude that there *is* no sensible rationale behind it. Just accept that even a feat as absurd as skipping two meals can set off an avalanche of complications.

Happily, there is a selection of relatively simple devices that will blunt the effectiveness and morph such a sacrifice into a diet rather than a defense. First, you must relentlessly divert your Target's concentration. Administer ADD. Exploit his inability to calibrate his brain so that it might converge upon the object of his fast. Clutter his mind with hundreds of nonessential concerns. Remember, the more formalized a fast, the more difficult it is for us to misdirect. Can you prompt him to forgo an opening and/or closing prayer? Can you at least help him postpone his inaugural prayer until the sixth, twelfth, or even the seventeenth hour?

We are helped enormously whenever a fast is enacted for convenience. Did your Target enjoy an early supper the previous evening? If so, can he be encouraged to avoid officially launching his act of abstinence until the next day, when he can justifiably believe that his sacrifice is already half concluded? Can the opening supplication itself be unfocused and cluttered? Keep in mind that the more generic we can make the fast, the more general will be its failure. Many cannot conceive enduring 24 hours of hunger pangs for a singular purpose. In addition, all fasts should address an infinitesimal inventory of issues. A fast's impact is generally diluted by obscuring its motives.

I realize that any brand of sincere sacrifice can harm our cause. Therefore, you must becloud the sincerity. Compromise the quality. And obfuscate the goal. Many in the Organization define fasting as bypassing two full meals. Mathematically this equals 24 hours, but in the petitioner's mind it need not equal any such thing! Meal times invariably differ, and a fast's duration should be correspondingly snipped. Your surest course is to promote anything that alleviates his level of discomfort. It's the voluntary *acceptance* of discomfort, affliction, and inconvenience which defines the act itself, and helps the petitioner to obtain some infinitesimal comprehension of the penultimate and ultimately depressing sacrifice undertaken by the Archenemy's Firstborn.

Finally, misdirect or obliterate the faith of the person fasting. The more narrowly you can define in the Target's mind the object of his efforts, the more disillusioned he will feel toward the result, and the less likely he will be in the future to habitually starve himself. The aim of a fast must always be seen in retrospect as an abject failure. Afterwards, suppress any and all inquiries he might make to the Archenemy to obtain supplementary illumination.

Now that my instructions are crystalline, I anticipate that your next dispatch will be an exculpatory screed showcasing your raving success. If I read anything that does not fully exonerate you from your former negligence, the consequences to you and your team will be indescribable. Do you hear me?— INDESCRIBABLE! (i.e., *not able to be described!*) Not that I couldn't describe the consequences if pressed. I simply prefer to keep them to myself. Do not misinterpret my words as an effort to milk the drama. I am merely allowing my visions of retribution to effervesce, hourly augmenting such musings to their murkiest . . . Okay, it's mostly to milk the drama.

Did you just cock your eyebrow at me?! I could flail you where you stand with a single twitch of my phalange! Ah, *devil-bless it!* Now I've spoiled my secret. But only partially. I assure you, you still have no idea of the full capacity of suffering that I am able to inflict. Ignore me at your *eternal peril!*

Your Fun-loving Führer,
MUCKWHIP

18

MY DEAR FROGKNOT,

You and your troop of imps are pathetic. I've grown fatigued dispensing my pearls of wisdom to a gaggle of half-wits! I've a mind to fry you all this very night in Cajun tempura with those little caramelized onions and a cilantro sprig (the spiritual variety of course, which is healthier for the digestion. Passes right through one's—*Do not misdirect my instructions with culinary distractions!*).

Couldn't penetrate the meeting for more than five minutes, eh? Not before the Opposition's forces tossed you out on your ears, eh?

You muttonheads make me hurl. This is *unbelievable!* Were you even aware that Mr. Moody was on his way OUT? It's perfectly true! His tempters had convinced him to vacate the premises before your praddling twosome even arrived! His plan was to hide out in the parking lot of the Piggly-Wiggly, waiting and watching until your Target and his companion pedaled off into the sunset. So explain to me why it entered Elder Hansen's mind to call Mr. Moody ten minutes before the appointment?! Moreover, why did you allow him to keep his investigator on the phone until his knuckles actually *knocked?* By then the brainless bootlicker was too flustered to do anything but invite them in!

I did note your vain attempt to trick your Target by having him dive into the lesson before hearing out Mr. Moody's full checklist of objections. Your effort was pitiful at best. Such brazen insensitivity should have sent Mr. Moody into a cyclone of incivility. *The tactic did not work!* We are momentarily stymied as to where to place the brunt of blame.

This hardly matters. You are in no position to point fingers at Mr. Moody's coterie of tempters. Your digits would only be devoured. Where was the interdepartmental cooperation about which I boasted so eloquently? What happened to our venerated confederacy of collusion? Moody just sat there *listening!* And that's the last thing you remember, right? Next thing you knew, you were face down on the pavement at the end of his hydrangea hedge.

In case you're interested, Elder Hansen never *did* finish his intended lesson. You see, Moody's wife joined the discussion. *What's that?!* Are your eyes backtracking to see if you read that correctly? Allow me to repeat: HIS WIFE JOINED THEM! It was one of the sneakiest attempts at counterespionage I've ever encountered. According to a reliable witness, who may or may not be the family cat, Elder Hansen approached Mrs. Moody in her studio and had the impertinence to invite her to join them. What, may I ask, happened to this boy's deficiency of confidence? We now suspect the Opposition may have *prompted* this invitation.

Do you comprehend what I'm saying?? Since when did your Target begin recognizing and *following* the Archenemy's prompts? Exactly what have you been doing the last few months, Frogknot? Have you logged a particle of progress whatsoever? By all gauges this alluvial grubworm is becoming more effective by the day. In light of these startling developments, I have no choice but to double the number of imps assigned to your Target. In addition to your other duties, you will also serve as regimental mucus-wiper. I'm also constrained to increase the patrols stalking Elder Lefler, Mr. Moody, and *Mrs.* Moody! Also, I'm reinforcing detachments assigned to their teenage children. We will take no more chances. This has become a Level One emergency. Any tempter suspected of lowering his guard will be relieved at once. And do not misconstrue the definition of "relieved." It means your mugs will be indelibly etched on the infernal menu. The hungry appetites of every fiend in the Lower Realms will fix squarely upon you.

The only reason you're not being fricasseed at this very moment is in recognition of the pittance of success you seem to have achieved with Elder Hansen's string-strumming neighbor. Still, I'd hardly call this a victory. Yes, he has rejected your elder's invitation to take the lessons, but why did their parting have to be so amicable? A lifelong assemblage of entrenched prejudices against the Organization were enthusiastically replaced. Mindsets were interminably softened. My fear now is that a very noxious seed has been planted—a seed that could prove our undoing at some future tempestivity of this musician's life.

Furthermore, your Target didn't display the slightest twinge of frustration. Such blunt force trauma to his oversized ego should have kicked him off balance for days. It should have been evident in his walk, his voice, his entire persona. Instead, he's striking out with the audacity of an African elephant. Your boy is becoming a *monster!* A genuflecting Godzilla who must be stopped at all costs!

So stoke an unquenchable fire in your bellies, my fellow tempters! Let your rage erupt into a firestorm of pyrotechnics! In short, make it *personal.* Benefits will be reinstated. Rewards multiplied. I'll throw in the latest computer tablet to the first tempter who penetrates that house the next time those pesky missionaries arrive on site. (No snide remarks about how we lack the necessary digits to operate such a device. Let me assure you, you'll have more fleshy fingers than you can count as soon as we win this infernal war and the earth is declared *ours*.)

I know, Frogknot, that you require no further persuasions than the ones I have just elucidated. Nevertheless, let me inform you that in your Target's hometown at this very minute a certain letter is being composed—one that should benefit our objectives prettily. Ah, yes—it's that infamous letter of which all elders with a hometown honey dread. Get ready, comrades! To savor this for all it's worth you must be relentless in your onslaught. *Go for the jugular!*

Your Masticating Manager,
MUCKWHIP

19

From: "Muckwhip" <muckwhip@waydownbelow.hel>

To: <frogknot@waydownbelow.hel>

Subject: happy day!

MY DEAR FROGKNOT,

Transferred?! What an inconceivably radiant stroke of luck! So you think you've been saved by the bell, eh, Frogknot? Perhaps you have. But before you exhale any full-throated sighs of relief let me remind you that all you've *really* done is pass the buck. The mess remains for others to try and sanitize. Don't think for a second that you've evaded accountability. You have not. Not by a long sight.

However, I will confess that I do feel some degree of pleasure at the sudden turn of events. I wish truly I could have seen his sour expression when he heard the announcement from mission headquarters. I trust your account well enough. Did he really argue with the president's assistant about the atrocious timing of this relocation? I'm chortling even now. These young shoats always think the world will fall desperately apart without them. And in this instance, I hope he's correct.

I'm confident that during his last encounter with Mr. Moody he relied far more upon his powers of persuasion than the promptings of the Archenemy's Spirit. I congratulate your cohort, Twillgill, for recognizing this pathetic reliance upon the arm of flesh. It allowed our speedy—if brief—penetration of the force field surrounding Moody's household. The tablet I was offering is deservedly his. We fully expect this episode of pride to reap well-deserved rewards. You see, Mr. and Mrs. Moody and their teenage offspring are clearly far more enamored of these sweet-talking elders than they are of the Organization itself. We understand news of your Target's disagreeable transfer was received with bitter disappointment. Therefore, the fiends in charge of the Moody family are under strict instructions to transform their disappointment into outright contempt at the earliest convenience. Contempt directed, of course, at the Organization.

We are not blind to the possibility that all this may be yet another tactic of the Opposition to ensnare this family more securely in its nets. Therefore a number of tempters in your platoon will remain with Elder Hansen's replacement. *You,* however, will pack your proverbial suitcase and make the move with your Target.

And what a favorable transfer it will be! Favorable for failure, that is. Do you realize the task they're entrusting to this mere amateur? They're granting him the authority to "open" an entirely new area for proselytizing—a hamlet that hasn't seen missionaries for nearly a decade. Not only that, but he'll be training a *greenie.* That's right—a tongue-wagging tadpole fresh from the MTC. And the Organization's leaders claim to be *inspired? Intoxicated* is more accurate. Oh, fellow tempters, this will be a *free-for-all!*

My only regret is that he will unfortunately miss—by a mere day—receipt of the nefarious letter that I mentioned earlier. No problem. It will be forwarded directly. And you can be sure that his new assignment will make its receipt all the more scrumptious and satisfying. This, along with his other pressures, will make his present burdens seem as oppressive as the weight of an aircraft carrier. But if I might be blunt, it won't be the challenge of opening a new area that will make his head spin. It will be the specter of his new companion.

Oh, I can't wait for you to meet him, Frogknot! His name is Calvin Cassell. This elder is a fine piece of work. Just ten months ago he was cruising Coeur d'Alene, Idaho with a six-pack of Coors riding shotgun. Only after his brother ratted him out to his bishop did he reluctantly agree to clean up his act. His parents presumed he'd confessed all to his Church leaders, though the most scandalous scraps he kept entirely hidden. Obviously certain regulations associated with "raising the bar" were summarily stretched. We relish the reality that these so-dubbed stricter standards have merely spawned a more shameless generation of liars.

Mr. Cassell begrudged his stateside assignment, and waffled in his resolve to serve until the night before departing Salt Lake International, when he secretly called his girlfriend to tell her he'd be home in a fortnight. So why is he here at *all*, you might inquire? You won't believe this. It's because he *wanted to see Florida!*

Wait, wait—it gets better! He actually *told* this to his mission president! Not only that, but he said that he had no idea if the Church was true and wasn't sure *if he wanted to find out!* The president asked him point blank if he'd like to board the next Southwest flight to Coeur d'Alene, to which the elder cheekily replied, "I promised my mother I'd give it a month."

After all that, our persevering president twirls him into the stewardship of your tenderfoot Target! Ah, you should have been there, Frogknot. I haven't laughed so uproariously in epochs. The timing couldn't have been better. Our resources are already taxed to the nth degree. We've assigned only a token taskforce to Elder Cassell; a dozen or so imps. I feel certain he'll never require a devil more, leaving us free to utilize remaining resources for shrewder purposes.

Elder Hansen has no idea what he's in for—in more ways than one. But enough chatter from me. You have a great deal of work to do. Your objectives haven't changed: disgruntlement, disenchantment, and disassociation. His Greyhound leaves at 4 p.m. and I expect each designated imp to be on board. He plans to sit beside a prospective convert, so you'll need to generate as much "white" noise as fiendishly possible.

If only I could stack the passenger list with equally energized proselytizers from a competing sect. Or comatose octogenarians. Or cardboard cutouts of *Twilight* characters. Or the smiling carcasses of crash dummies . . .

Sorry, I lost my train of thought. *Carry on!*

Your Indefatigable Instructor,
MUCKWHIP

20

From: "Muckwhip" <muckwhip@waydownbelow.hel>
To: <frogknot@waydownbelow.hel>
Subject: dear john

MY DEAR FROGKNOT,

He got it, eh? It's about time. My, how postal services have improved! I must confess, Frogknot, I've looked forward to this event with such conniving anticipation for so long that I'm feeling a bit of a letdown. Could my fantasies ever truly become the reality? Please offer up a comprehensive blow-by-blow in your next report so that I might immerse myself in an ablution of gloating.

In particular I'd like to know his reaction when he read the line, *"I will always hold a special place in my heart for you, Stuart, but Gordon seems to love me more than any man I've ever known, and I'm afraid if I let him go, I'll regret it for the rest of my life."* Now that's *literature!* Pure poetry. She does know how to twist the knife, doesn't she? She actually thought she was being *sensitive,* letting him down easy. What an airhead! Unquestionably incapable of dispensing to her brain an appropriate amount of oxygen. If my calculations are correct, this letter will effectively pulverize Elder Hansen. He'll become a broken man. Like a needle in a balloon, I expect every ounce of ambition, valor, and exuberance to slowly whistle free from his bloated intestinal tract. Much of this, of course, depends upon *you*. I've seen missionaries stagger away from such a correspondence little more than walking zombies, having no concern for future events, and no longer caring about the failure or success of the work. In a flash these once-stalwart representatives of the Archenemy are empty husks onerously awaiting the end of their internment. Their favorite pastime becomes crossing off days on the calendar, and regretting every wasted moment in the Archenemy's employ.

It's time to start your most aggressive campaign of spiritual conflagration. Begin by urging Elder Hansen to reject the most fundamental mission rules. Instead of hitting the snooze button on the alarm, have him yank the cord from the wall and spike the appliance against the floor. Companionship and personal study are out of the question. If he *must* leave his apartment, let it not be a moment before noon. The day's schedule should consist of long, unproductive visits to the homes of willing members, wherein subjects are addressed that have nothing to do with flushing out converts. If you'd like, you might persuade him to pine on and on about his broken heart.

Let me suggest a tricky, but rewarding tactic—but only if it can be skillfully and thoughtfully executed. Entice him to befriend one or more of the *less* active members in the local ward and move in. That's right. For multiple hours a day he should practically take up residence. It's easy enough to convince a missionary that he's doing the "Lord's work" in such circumstances. He must rationalize that he is engaged in a sincere effort to reform a renegade. The selection is critical. Someone who is solitary, self-absorbed, and with a caboodle of similar interests or vices. Your Target must determine that redefining mission rules is suddenly incumbent. Thus, so long as he is promoting reactivation, he can simultaneously enjoy countless hours of ESPN, World of Warcraft, or Rodgers and Hammerstein.

Dinner appointments should always masticate considerably more time than what is allocated. Spur him back to his domicile an hour early. Or several hours late. Whichever suits the occasion. As the DL phones for weekly stats, teach your Target to excel in the fine art of fudging. For instance, any chat with an arbitrary biped, even if they discuss the excellence of his azaleas, should always be check-marked as a theological discourse.

As we previously discussed, no one will be more supportive of such disobedience than his current companion. In fact, Elder Cassell might serve as the *instigator*—the author of idleness, the mastermind of mischief. If such transpires, consider refining your approach. Instead of scattering seeds of contention betwixt them, cultivate the bonds of friendship. Partners in crime, if you will. Send them to the cinema. Make fishing gear available and convey them to the catfish pond. Have you noted that Universal Studios and Disney World are but a few measly miles outside of mission boundaries? Now that your Target is driving an automobile, why not entice them to undertake a thrilling "expedition"?—a P-day to end all P-days!

But of course, the *pièce de rèsistance* would be for you to massage your Target into frequenting the apartment of any of this town's flirtatious *ingénues*. He's particularly vulnerable to female attention right now. The effects of an attractive floozy upon a disgraced and discarded elder can be more paralyzing than kryptonite.

The delicious evil that can be concocted by two missionaries of the same rebellious ilk is a lovely spectacle to behold. Various youth in the local branch may even decide against serving missions. (Their parents may even sympathize after witnessing the antics of certain full-time proselytizers!) There are few icons of the Organization more familiar to everyday folks than an LDS elder in his white shirt and tie.

Local perceptions might not recover for decades. Some affected parties may *never* recover. Generations yet unborn will reap the repercussions of transgressions left smoldering if you will only capitalize on a few vital moments. It's in your hands, Frogknot. Don't drop the ball. Or the ball will most assuredly drop on you.

I'm sure you've heard that the situation in your Target's previous area has not improved. Elder Hansen's replacement is no less obnoxious, underhanded, and "protected" than his predecessor. In other words, he reeks of the Archenemy's Spirit. My legions can't seem to orchestrate an attack from any angle. Unless you score an impressive victory in your present assignment, another sojourn in the Re-education Camp for Incompetent Tempters will be penciled onto your agenda. Trust me, you'll think your last visit was a VIP pleasure cruise compared to what awaits. Yes, it does include attentive room service. Just not the kind that you might have imagined.

Your Compassionate Concierge,
MUCKWHIP

21

From: "Muckwhip" <muckwhip@waydownbelow.hel>
To: <frogknot@waydownbelow.hel>
Subject: unbelievable!

MY DEAR FROGKNOT,

Tell me I did not read your last communiqué correctly. Tell me I've incorrectly interpreted the whole metagrobolized mess! What do you *mean* your Target has gone back to work!? What do you *mean* he's teaching several new families? This is inconceivable! What nincompoop would actually believe that the best remedy for heartache and pain is to throw oneself more earnestly into the Archenemy's service? I wouldn't have thought *anyone*—particularly a missionary—was moronic enough to fall for such vapid dime-store nonsense.

What's WRONG with this guy!?

Not only this, but the imps in charge of his companion, Elder Cassell, report that they're suffering interference whenever they try to attack. Did you hear what I said? *Elder Cassell!* He's acting like-like . . . like an *elder!* He's following your Target's lead at every turn. What in blundering blazes is going on over there? Have you idiots taken permanent leave of your senses? Are you *begging* to be flailed, bludgeoned, and disemboweled?

I've received a dispatch that may explain the interference with Elder Cassell. But I refuse to believe it's the *only* explanation. It makes no sense! Apparently his family back home—especially his lunatic mother—prays for his welfare *continually*. Not just weekly or nightly, but *every time they get on their knees!* Fasting too. And with excessive, maniacal, and psychotic determination. Despite this elder's diabolical attitude, despite his overabundant weaknesses, despite his complete lack of preparation for this undertaking, *the Archenemy is aiding and protecting him anyway!*

It's an outrage! It's unjust! Unconscionable! So typical of the Opposition's profligate hypocrisy! The boy shouldn't even *be* on a mission! His state of repentance is incomplete! We should have access to every facet of this reprobate's disposition. *Those are the rules!* Such statutes have been in place since time immemorial! How can we be expected to tally triumphs if the Archenemy doesn't *play fair?* That's it. I'm filing a formal, unequivocal complaint. Not sure yet what department receives these particular protests, *but I'm filing it anyway!*

Don't think that this excuses *you*, you insubordinate leech. You and your compatriots have exactly twenty-four hours— no, no—sixty minutes! *No, no—sixty seconds!*—to persuade me that I shouldn't massacre the entire lot of you. Can't come up with anything? Then *I'll* give you a reason. Because I have no desire this evening to incur repeated visits to the gagatorium!

As far as Elder Cassell, we will simply wait him out. Our patience will be unrelenting. His past *will* catch up to him. I assure you, we'll eventually hack a breach in his fortifications. In the end, it's all about *physics*. And no homo sapiens can prevail *in perpetuity* without enlisting incontestable repentance.

So I'll give you one last chance, Frogknot. One last opportunity to entice your Target into committing a bona fide transgression. Otherwise I'll personally see you dragged back to the Re-education Camp by your tongue. In case you misinterpret my meaning, this success must materialize *before* he returns to his old area to participate in the baptism of the Moody family. Oh, yes! Did you think I hadn't heard the news? I'm *fully* aware that the entire Moody ménage has committed to joining the Organization. I'm *fully* aware that the father has requested Elder Hansen to perform the ordinance, and *fully* aware that the mission president has approved the request. I've snatched myself bald, screamed myself hoarse, and bitten my nails to the knuckle over this debacle.

Do you hear what I'm telling you? Read my lips—NO NEW DISASTERS! I'll not tolerate even one more disappointment regarding this Target. It's a matter of death and hell! Are you myrmidons or are you mice?! You and your comrades must be willing to stretch yourselves to the utmost periphery of your abilities and *beyond* or each of you will baste in the hottest flames Hell has ever ignited. *I exaggerate not!* The very kingdom of our infernal father is at stake. And I will not accept one jot or tittle of redirected blame for your incomprehensible imbecility.

So become the ravenous wolf that you are, Frogknot. The claw-slashing grizzly. The bone-crunching barracuda. I know it's in you. Reach down into the cold, black recesses of whatever you call a heart and make this the single most important objective of your forgettable career. I still feel assured that if you hunger for victory voraciously enough, you *will* achieve it. That's right, my apprentice. I haven't lost confidence in you. Just patience and leniency. Although, in case you're wondering, I never had much of either to begin with.

Your Maleficent Mentor,
MUCKWHIP

22

MY DEAR, SWEET, INCOMPETENT FROGKNOT,

You know the routine.

Pack your things (which consists of only your sorry backside), haul yourself down to the local depot, stand alongside the track, extend your tongue, and await my envoy of henchmen to snag it with their hooks as they pass on a speeding train. They will drag you, bouncing and gagging, to your next tour of indoctrination in the lowest recesses of the Re-education Camp for Incompetent Tempters. The teary-eyed warden claims that he misses you very much. I have requested that he make your stay more memorable than before. *Considerably* more memorable.

As you may have guessed, you're not going alone. Every fiend currently in Elder Hansen's entourage will join you. For your pathetic negligence, I'm replacing the entire lot of you with fresh, eager recruits who will most certainly make better progress. My only regret is that I didn't replace you earlier. As I understand it, not only did your Target successfully baptize every member of the Moody household in his last area, he has

committed for baptism two completely new investigators—
one of whom was the college student he sat beside on the bus
during his last transfer!

You've left in your wake such an incomprehensible
ruination that my new squadron of tempters isn't exactly sure
where to begin. Do you realize what you have done? Do you
realize the breadth of your failure? There are now *sentries*
guarding Elder Hansen's every waking moment—sentries
from the Archenemy's very presence! And not just while he's
awake. They stand guard at his bedside, their blinding
immanence repelling every phalanx and sortie we send against
them. We can hardly *see* the boy anymore, to say nothing of
getting near him.

Your replacements are little more than muskrats seeking
for chinks in the titanium-lined moat of an impenetrable
fortalice. But don't worry, my dear apprentice. They'll find his
flaws. Oh, they'll find them. And in the end, Elder Stuart
Hansen will grovel like a slime-slicked mealworm and beg for
relief. This is my personal guarantee to our infernal father. I've
staked my spotless reputation upon it.

Perhaps your most grievous blunder pertains to what has
become of his companion. In case you're curious, the imps in
charge of Elder Cassell are *also* joining you. Every tooth in
every department in the Lower Realms is gnashing. This is
Calvin Cassell for misery's sake!—champion and advocate of
hellish happenstances his entire adolescence! Now we fear this
cockroach might actually be *converted!*

Yes, he's confessed everything to his mission president. Yes,
it's been decided that he must return home as part of his
repentance and reparations. But don't you *get it?* In the case
of Calvin Cassell, this is the worst possible news that might
have reached my auriculars! He might now consider himself
one of them! An affiliate of the Organization! And since your
Target is to blame for awakening his personal accountability,

so, by default, are *you*. If not for your Target's example, Elder Cassell would *still* be wreaking rapturous havoc for our benefit and merriment.

This was an inexcusable miscalculation on your part! Our minions are working around the clock even now to discover some obscure contrivance that will help us to recapture the original, pure (or rather, purely *corrupt*) Calvin Cassell forevermore. Despite his willingness to endure such shameful consequences, he is actually relieved! Hopeful! Rejoicing! He must be slapped out of this spiritual stupor before we are forced to totally cancel his imminent arrival at our department's butcher shop. I'd already put in a pre-order for a rump roast!

In time I'm sure you'll agree that your punishments are wholly deserved. After all, you have failed at one of the most important assignments in all the Dominion of Discord. This is ground zero. The stakes are too high. The prize too sweet. We cannot and *will* not abdicate this fight. And in case you're befuddled by the score card, let me remind you that we *are* winning. Never mind your terrible blunders. Never mind the overwhelming forces that continue to oppress us. Our eventual victory is assured. It will be ours by a landslide. *So what* if the Archenemy appears more colossal and commanding with each passing moment? It's all an illusion. We're quite certain. He does it with mirrors. If He were *really* so powerful, do you think our infernal father would compel us to fight in vain? Our fearless leader knows *exactly* what he's doing. Of that I'm sure. Yes, *infinitely* sure!

But he can't do it alone. (Strike that. Oh, sorry. I realize we're not allowed to erase. Of course our infernal father *could* do it alone if he so desired. He makes that point perfectly clear. We're only allowed to assist in the Archenemy's undoing by virtue of our commander's immeasurable good graces. Many pardons!) Nevertheless, it is our venerable *duty* to strive with all our might, mind, and strength to contain this pestilence of elders—or devour each other trying! We'll double, triple, *octuple* the guard if we have to. There's no limit to the resources our Central Office is willing to commit. We cannot allow another acre of ground to be dedicated to the Organization's infestation. Leaders of nations must slam their doors. The Church's reputation must be tarnished at every opportunity. As has always occurred throughout history, the Organization must be encouraged to collapse from within. And as always, our overwhelming success will be revealed in the strangled efforts of its missionaries. We *will* vanquish!

Unfortunately, it will be some time before you again have a front row seat at this ongoing contest. Bide your time, Frogknot. And learn well. If you are still sane upon your release (and there's a high probability that you will not be) your next assignment will be the most important of all.

In spite of all that you've experienced, there remains one theatre of operation more critical than even the one wherein you've been grappling. This battlefront will unquestionably demand all of your energies for the remainder of your tenure in my department. If you fail at this, there *is* no re-education. Only basting and roasting. And I find that the stronger the Organization gets, the hungrier I become.

Your Insatiable Eminence,
MUCKWHIP

Part III:

AGAINST FAMILIES

23

From: "Muckwhip" <muckwhip@waydownbelow.hel>
To: <frogknot@waydownbelow.hel>
Subject: hello?

FROGKNOT?

Are you in there? I have been asked not to speak to you using words that have more than one or two syllables. (Sorry about the word *syllables*.) They say you're doing much better, yes? Not as much twitching or drooling. This is good to hear. I have high hopes that you will return to active duty very soon. Does this excite you? I'm sure it does. Until then, you just keep getting better. Okie-dokey?

I just wanted to tell you that Stuart Hansen is home from his mission now. Do you remember Mr. Hansen? That's right. Your Target from before. Exactly. The one you failed so badly to tempt and destroy. Shaking again, are we? Sorry. My fault. I won't get into that now. I'll just give you a brief update on what's happened since you left.

As I said, he's home now. His mission was . . . How shall I put it? . . . not a chipper time for us. Your team wasn't the only one we had to drag off by their tongues. There were others. But all that's behind us now. He was released last week. His homecoming is set for Sunday. His mantle is removed. Simply put, he's like the rest of them again. At least for our purposes. And like so many before him, his greatest struggle for the next while is something called "spiritual withdrawal." Getting back into the groove, so to speak. A silly ailment, really. But they all seem to go through it. We build on it, of course, by telling them that they are correct to think that they're worthless. That they no longer serve any useful purpose. Sadly, this feeling ends sooner than we'd like.

We have much success telling many to just stop going to church at this point. The shift from a life of strict routine and clear goals to one of common cares is too much to handle. We plan to pursue this course with your Target as well. With any luck, by the time you're back on the job, he will look upon his two years in the field as a massive theological overload. (Too many syllables again? Sorry. I'll return to shorter words.) He'll decide he needs a long break from fasting, prayer, scripture—from the whole church scene altogether. We will then display a whole host of worldly pleasures that he has denied himself for far too long.

Just watch, Frogknot. You might think that two years focused on one single purpose would make these schmucks harder to tempt. Not so. Often the "loss of spirit" they feel makes them much prepped for molding. Unless they sink their teeth into some sort of prime service to aid in the transition, their emptiness can turn to self-indulgence, and self-indulgence to sin (devil bless those syllables!).

There's one more matter I must mention. Do you recall his old girlfriend, Traci Paxton? The self-righteous prude—yes, that's right. Very odd stuff to report there. It's true that she sent him a ruthless Dear John. But as luck would have it, plans did not work out with her beau. Four weeks before the wedding, she called it off. Something about not being able to trust him. You see, he had an old flame. The two chose to have one last date and, well . . . we took over from there. Score a big one for us, eh? A classic. You should have been there. I think you were still being pureed by Mr. Juiceman at the time. Oh well. Anyhoo, your Target heard about her botched wedding plans the day he got home. He thought about calling her—just to offer support, or so I'm told. To his credit (that is to say, to *our* credit) pride took over and he set the phone aside. Good thing, too. Rumor has it that she thinks about him too. She knows that he's home now. She feels guilty that she did not meet him at the airport. We'll do all that we can to expand such guilt and toss in a little shame to boot. The truth is, if these two meet up again, it would be very bad. They must be kept apart. You know the saying: To forgive is childish, to err divine. We've done the math, and a union between this couple could prove quite yucky. At least we're not willing to take any chances.

Instead, we're helping him meet some nice, worldly women. You know the type. Brainless. All about self. He seems set on going back to his old hobby of guitar strumming and song writing at the moment. We all know the breed of airheads who loiter among those who frequent *that* métier. One of our pretty, pretty allies should have her hooks in him soon enough.

Alas, I've rambled too long. It appears that your eyes are starting to glaze. I'm told that when and if you recover, you'll not only have renewed, seething fierceness to help you, but nimble street smarts. You'll need them both if you're to be of any use to me. I expect you to become a "fiend machine." An android-like entity with no stray thought beyond munching the souls to whom you are assigned. Can you be that for me, Froggie, ol' chum? I knew you could. I sooo look forward to having you back. No rush. The most important thing is that you return to us happy and whole. Or at least able and ready. I have, however, told the imps in charge of your healing that if you're not prepped by the weekend, they'll take your place at the reform home. I suspect they got my oh-so-subtle meaning.

Now mop up that drool and *heal*, my boy! *Heal!*

Your Sympathetic Superior,
MUCKWHIP

24

From: "Muckwhip" <muckwhip@waydownbelow.hel>
To: <frogknot@waydownbelow.hel>
Subject: in form

MY DEAR FROGKNOT,

Good to again see your bright, shining face, my esteemed and talented apprentice! And not a moment too soon. If you'll pardon me, I'll skip the usual pleasantries to which I am accustomed when someone of whom I am so fond returns to the fold. Nor is there time for you to be formally introduced to your new platoon of tempters. (Yes, you're still very much a part of a *team*.) We have a bit of an emergency that requires your urgent attention.

She came to the homecoming! Can you believe it? She was there when he stood at the pulpit during sacrament meeting to rattle off his mission memoirs. How she swallowed her hairball of pride and subjected herself to such an exhibition is beyond us. She did it, nonetheless, and our principal focus right now is damage control. He noticed her straightway, of course, and beelined toward the pew where she was sitting the instant the meeting concluded.

At first we were relieved that she vacated the building in all the confusion, but this departure had a peculiar effect upon the mind of Mr. Hansen. He couldn't stop thinking about her. His ruminations became a bubbling obsession and by day's end he was sending her text messages. The following night the *dummkopf* dialed her cell number. What we'd hoped would become a blood-thirsty argument mutated into a four-hour blab-a-thon. Now the couple has set their sights on a lunch date later this week.

All rightie, then! Lock and load, gentlemen! Let them try to obstruct our efforts at sabotage! We realize there's little we can do to prevent this luncheon. Therefore our strategy must be to transform this meal into ultimate carnage and mayhem. This "date" must be injected with as much sarcasm and priggishness as possible. This, we hope, will effectively squelch any sparks of romance. Every tempter in your squadron is commanded to shout brutal reminders into his ear about how she forced his heart through a paper shredder. How she obliterated his emotions with an Uzi! This lunch must lay a foundation of unprecedented loathing!

You might wonder why we have such a keen interest in smothering this relationship. After all, most of these sniveling mortals will eventually settle into matrimony. The answer is not abstruse. We oppose it because these two pompous parasites are *worthy*. If we do not toss in the customary monkey wrench, the chances that this marriage will be solemnized in one of those abominable temples are depressingly high. Such a union is *never* acceptable. It is frightening. It is ominous. It thwarts everything our infernal father has stood against from the inception of time. Namely: keeping these slimy upstarts from climbing out of the primordial abyss. Even when such a ceremony is performed, the promise of eternal bliss is never *guaranteed*. Thankfully for us, it is subject to the keeping of certain covenants. Nevertheless it becomes a sanctioned *possibility*. This is dreadful enough.

Do you realize what an eternal marriage could mean? It means this couple can now procure a first-class passport to become like *Him*. That's right. A Golden Ticket to exaltation. What's more, the Archenemy has proclaimed that striving to secure such a ceremony is a *commandment*—the most underhanded and conniving commandment ever instituted. We despise temple unions with every strand of curlicue hair on our backs. For one thing, we never get an invitation. Nor are we allowed to crash the party. But that is beside the point.

Since a temple marriage is the only way for *homo sapiens* to become like the Archenemy and His Son and be forever reunited with Him in His grossly overrated celestial cesspool, it's only natural that all our strategies, from start to finish, focus upon preventing or frustrating this singular event.

Thwart a celestial marriage and you stop the creature dead in his tracks. It's the apex of everything we detest. We achieve no greater victory than if we torpedo this *Titanic* and sink it to the bottom of the Marianas Trench. But it must be a *resounding* victory. In other words, we must allow the possibility to float like an intangible dream just before your Target's proboscis—just *millimeters* from his eternal grasp. After all, if a Target never has the opportunity to have those silly temple "blessings" bestowed, either because of geographical limitations or because no legitimate proposal was ever forthcoming, we cannot claim credit. Our rewards are suddenly relegated to a category of unharvested hopes. Unwitting ignorance and a lack of opportunity are unfortunately judged in the Target's favor. It's a reprehensible loophole!

Thus, the opportunity must be dangling directly before the Target's noodle, and in Mr. Hansen's case—as with most males—it most definitely is. He has no excuses. The only victory sweeter than dismantling temple attendance is enticing your Target to continue such visits after slipping into transgression. Corrosive iniquity or immorality. We'll discuss this objective in greater detail down the road. For now we must foil and confound the dynamics of this upcoming luncheon. Your Target is still smarting over his in-your-face rejection while serving in the mission field.

In certain ways he's like a shaken can of carbonation. What he'd *really* like to do at this reunion is grab her by the lapel and explode in her face—tell her off but *good!* Make her feel some fraction of the excruciating pain that he endured for all those months. We like this. All the motivations for this are already in place. All we have to do is "pop" the tab.

To make this happen there has to be a concerted effort betwixt your team and the minions in charge of Miss Paxton. Her tempters have been carefully instructed to spur her toward vigorously defending her technique for dumping him. This should be more than adequate. Let her justify it all as the "right thing to have done at the time." That's when we'll hit the detonator.

What a beautiful thing if this unsightly shindig can be morphed into a tearful shouting match, with one person storming out on the other. Then we can nip this nonsense in the bud and return to our former tactic of introducing him to some of our more conniving missies who couldn't distinguish morality from Milk Duds.

I trust your hatred of Mr. Hansen hasn't diminished. After all, if any soul deserves the blame for your tortures and trauma, it's your incorrigible Target. Time for a little payback, wouldn't you say? It's your last chance. I assure you, Frogknot, he's still very much yours for the barbecuing. If you can finally succeed in destroying him in this critical phase, I promise you won't have to share this meal with anyone. Every tidbit and morsel will be yours. Just as the opposite outcome will make you mine for the marinating.

It's fabulous to be working together again, isn't it? Oh how I've missed you, my Froggie! I assure you, my heartfelt devotions haven't subsided in the least. Nor has my opinion of your capabilities. I must say that I often think of you more like your father than as your undisputed superior. And not only because, like many fathers, I have a distinct inclination to eat my young. Nay, that's but a very small part of it. I assure you my sentiments extend much deeper into my viscera. Now go and make me proud! (Sniff!)

Your Emotional Imperialist,
MUCKWHIP

25

From: "Muckwhip" <muckwhip@waydownbelow.hel>
To: <frogknot@waydownbelow.hel>
Subject: WHAT?!

MY DEAR FROGKNOT,

Engaged!? After *three weeks?* Don't people take the time to get to *know* each other anymore? Discover each other's faults? Grow on each other's nerves? Experiment with forbidden taboos? What's *happening* to the young people of today?! Too much texting. Too many reality shows. Wait a sec. Many of those industries work for us. Never mind.

These circumstances have become so syrupy-sweet that I taste vomit every time I think about it. What became of all that pent-up bitterness and schemes for psychological vengeance? Yes, I understand that she presented a plausible argument for being contrite and acting so cockamamie and bla, bla, bla. But this is *male ego* we're talking about! No real man forgives so easily after being spurned—not the way *he* was spurned. Tell him what a wimp he is, Frogknot. Shout it in his ear. *Wuss! Weakling! Whey-faced quiche-crunching chipmunk!*

Mr. Hansen hasn't even established decent employment! How could he possibly support a litter of packrats? Whisper it to him. Whisper it over and over. Tell him how tying the knot at this juncture is the same as passing a sentence of death upon his aspirations to be a professional musician. Tell him he's not *ready* to wear these kinds of shackles. Love in his present condition of poverty could only spell disaster. They *all* cave to this brand of pressure! We can frequently sucker them to eschew commitment for decades!

I also hear that they've tentatively set the date for September—only a few short months in the future! This is totally unacceptable. Not only is my calendar booked that week (I'm collaborating with a screenwriter on yet another celluloid cavalcade of teenage debauchery. Hooray for Hollywood!), but since both of these individuals reside in the same hometown and see each other daily, it's imperative to draw out this engagement much like a presidential campaign season. Need I explain why? Of course not. But for my own entertainment, I'll explain anyway.

It's because they're "human." How I adore that definition in this context! It's the only honest definition these belching brutes ever attach to themselves. It acknowledges their very nature—weak, fallible, untrustworthy, obstreperous, corrupt. In short, carnal, sensual and "devilish" (as if they could ever be worthy of that label! But to their credit, imitation *is* the highest form of flattery).

Each minute that these morons spend in each other's presence increases the likelihood that physical affection will cross boundaries that will disqualify them from temple worthiness. Time in this situation is our bosom buddy, our cherished friend. Why haven't you pressed the argument that because they got engaged so quickly, they need a few extra months to "get to know one another"?

I so deeply prize this phase, particularly when it regards an engaged twosome. How can they think it's possible to really know every facet of someone's character in such a brief span? This is when twitterpation and hormones and rose-colored bifocals blur *everything*. Still, the debate is so weighted in our favor. It's so suited to common sense. "Yes!" you must mutter. "By all means! Get to know one another! Be absolutely certain that you're doing the *right thing*." But be wary, Frogknot. Do not allow this to become a spiritual question. It must remain a Gordian knot that can only be untangled with *time*. Heaps and gobs and oodles of it.

The truth is that most of these muttonheads—even after adhering to the strictest guidelines by selecting someone of their own faith, temperament, humor, etc.,—will uncover umpteen incompatibilities as soon as they are wedded. Just the fact that they are male and female makes them supremely incompatible from the outset. But they must never interpret it this way. Of late the wisdom of the world has become enormously helpful in convincing these young miscreants that one of the foremost areas wherein compatibility is paramount is in matters of intimacy. What a howler! One day I'll explain how this deception is advantageous both before marriage and *after*.

Keep them inching closer to the line of immorality, Frogknot—ever closer. Kissing must lead to necking, necking to petting, etc., etc. With each phase the downward spiral only steepens, until at last you land a prize more succulent than a perfectly marbled filet mignon. After all, they're engaged, right?! Isn't it just a matter of weeks before they bask in the bliss of honeymoon intimacy every blessed day and night? What difference will it really make if they start to indulge a tad early?— whether it be a few scanty weeks, days, or even *hours?* You'd be surprised what rationalizations we can help to gain traction in the crucible of curiosity. All in the "heat" of being "human."

But if you think your rewards can't get any more tantalizing, you're wrong. To *really* top this off with a maraschino, let them ensnare themselves in immorality, and then follow through with the temple sealing *anyway!* Oh, the opportunities you will reap! Defenses will evaporate. Protections will be pulverized.

And your possibilities for promotion will extend to the highest levels of the Infernal Realm.

However, according to our best calculations, this particular outcome is not very likely. The most predictable consequence if they slide into sin is actually a dissolution of their engagement. You see, as soon as the fires of passion subside, shame, disrespect, and distrust are sure to follow. Such remorse may in fact display itself most dramatically upon the features of Miss Paxton. After all, similar misdeeds on the part of her previous fiancée vaporized all of her prior visions of marital happiness and tranquility. If she cannot feel assured that her current fiancée is superior to her last, we feel certain she will *not* follow through with the ceremony. And in this case, this wouldn't be such a bad outcome at all!

After the fireworks of bitterness and estrangement, your first concern will be—as always—repentance. Because your Target is a temple-endowed elder, we anticipate that the road back to full fellowship in the Organization will be akin to a foot-crossing of the Sahara. And as ever, your methods of manipulation are precisely the same: before the sin, assuage him that repentance is a *cinch*. Afterwards, that it's an algebraic *impossibility*.

Ah, but listen to me prattle on. I speak as if the sin has already been committed. You still have an abundance of work ahead of you. Put the pedal to the metal, my blessed myrmidon! Oh, and if you think your prospects for milking your Target's acrimony over Miss Paxton's previous spurning have passed, think again. Such rancor will continue to effervesce beneath the surface for a long while, just waiting for the perfect opportunity to combust. Even if we fail to capitalize upon such simmering antipathy before the wedding, we'll have a field day with it thereafter. Do you doubt my appraisal? Just watch and wait.

Your Perspicacious Potentate,
MUCKWHIP

26

From: "Muckwhip" <muckwhip@waydownbelow.hel>
To: <frogknot@waydownbelow.hel>
Subject: newlyweds

MY DEAR FROGKNOT,

This day is dark.

Caliginous as charcoal. Murky as primordial muck. Barren as the most tenebrous black hole. A day so sodden with gloom that all of the Infernal Realms paused for one oppressive moment and mourned to the depths of their innermost bowels. *That disgusting pair of curs prevailed!* They've outmaneuvered your every effort, obstructed your subtlest whisperings, and muzzled your most cacophonous screams. You'd be impaled on my fork right now, Frogknot, if not for the technicality that you have so recently returned to active duty. As it is, I'm feasting on a stew that includes the better part of your comrades, slurping them up like slithering strands of spaghetti.

How did it feel to watch them enter that place, that impregnable fortress, squished on all sides by beloved family and friends with their Aspartame smiles—including *both* of your Target's parents!? Did you cringe with shame as you watched them in their wedding-day bib-and-tucker, both of them radiating that terrible, toxic glow of untainted purity? Did you disgorge in revulsion, knowing they each fully *deserved* to be there? That they'd swiped the prize in *spite* of you? Despite all your ill-timed and incompetent efforts?

More than two decades of hard-fought campaigning— endeavors that utilized our most adroit operatives and most lethal armaments—comes into full account this day. And what, pray tell, do we have to show for it? So precious little I'd need an electron microscope to detect it.

They are *sealed*, Frogknot! I shudder to contemplate the full significance of that word. *Sealed* to inherit all that the Archenemy hath. *Sealed* to receive powers and honors treacherously deprived from us for the foreseeable future. *Sealed* to obtain all the glories that *should* have been—and one day *will* be—ours. It's so scandalously unfair! So egregiously unjust that these sweat-exuding primates, comprised of 96% water and 4% mud, should find themselves exalted to receive as permanent quarters the finest real estate in the quadrant! What about *us?* The wisest, wittiest, and most qualified entities in all of creation? Are we just expected to roll over and accept this injustice? Are we to allow the riches of the universe to be squandered upon sniffling, salivating wretches like Mr. and Mrs. Stuart Hansen?

Think again, dear hearts! A paltry ceremony behind granite walls will not change the ultimate outcome of this war. We are the champions of practicality, not the executors of the kind of superficial tripe peddled by the Archenemy and His legions. We have been *wronged*, compatriots! Since we fight for a superior cause, we can fully expect that the tides of power *will* eventually shift in our favor. What other rational conclusion can an intelligent being draw?

So enjoy your overpriced honeymoon in Cabo San Lucas, Mr. and Mrs. Hansen—and catch a little Montezuma's Revenge while you're at it! One day soon all your counterfeit and fleeting happiness will become meaningless as the true inheritors of this earth plant their interminable flag.

Of course I'm kidding about the "enjoy" part, Frogknot. Actually, I expect you to be on hand every moment, endeavoring to sabotage their festivities. This may seem difficult at first, as the Archenemy's Spirit is often pervasive in the initial tenure of worthy newlyweds. Be assured that you will upset their tranquility and trigger their hot buttons of disharmony soon enough. All their lives they've fostered certain expectations with regard to honeymoons—expectations celebrated by song, legend, and prime-time television. The new wife especially has always fantasized that her honeymoon would inaugurate a kind of flower-petal-strewn Utopia, that for an uninterrupted spell she would luxuriate in the company of a man whose character is marked by tender selflessness, attention affixed to her every need, and worshipping her every toenail. He, on the other hand, is expecting nothing less than a willing Aphrodite whose very existence eagerly and vigorously complies with pleasing his every whim.

These expectations will shatter soon enough without much prodding from you. It always surprises the male how quickly he becomes distracted and eager to embark upon other adventures. Urge him to suggest a day of deep-sea fishing rather than remaining cloistered in their tiny hotel room. After all, how often will they visit a marlin angler's paradise like Cabo? I assure you, she'll remember such a thoughtless misdemeanor long after their 50th wedding anniversary, and she'll remind him at every awkward opportunity. Let this be the beginning of Mr. Hansen's consternation regarding the temperament of brides. Might as well set our strategic time bombs for detonation right from the get-go.

From now on, Frogknot, all your blitzkriegs must be choreographed in perfect harmony with whatever circumstances might be affecting his partner. Demolishing a marriage is a meticulously orchestrated campaign. We exploit every opening with symphonic precision. You will simultaneously memorize *her* weaknesses as you take advantage of his. This will ensure that their flaws chafe against one another like sandpaper grinding against the grain.

Massacring this marriage is now your principal occupation. None of the promises made or oaths pronounced in that terrible temple will come to pass unless those endowed abide by the covenants made therein. Our advantage is that his accountability is now more imposing. You must employ deception, manipulation, pride, vanity, intolerance, and disloyalty—either contemplated or consummated—to precipitate this union's untimely end. No failure can compensate for success in the home. Repeat this in your cerebellum every single day. Although we may have missed our opportunity to nuke the nuptials, there are still a multitude of available perks—some of a particularly delectable variety—that can be earned by convincing this eternal couple to toss aside all their petty covenants in favor of narcissistic pursuits.

Am I also correct in saying that both the engagement party and the honeymoon bash were procured on credit? This is excellent. A wonderful foundation to build upon. And thanks to that imp-inspired phenomenon known as interest, family debts should accrue quite nicely.

Now if you'll excuse me, your former team leader is trying to wriggle off my fork. The silly slug. How far does he think he'd get drenched in Béarnaise?

Your Garrulous Gourmet,
MUCKWHIP

27

From: "Muckwhip" <muckwhip@waydownbelow.hel>
To: <frogknot@waydownbelow.hel>
Subject: back to basics

MY DEAR FROGKNOT,

I'm still scratching my noggin, apprentice. I find it astonishing how you are capable of speaking, scribbling, or communicating at *all* considering that your BRAIN is on PERMANENT VACATION inside the BAJORAN WORMHOLE!

I read your recent proposal on resources required for decimating the Hansen household. Admittedly, there were a few salient points, particularly those ideas that you lifted verbatim from my *own* proposal some centuries ago regarding invalidating the nuptials of Henry VIII and Anne Boleyn. Despite the unlikelihood that anyone is going to lop off their mate's head, your budget is obscenely extravagant. Perhaps if you eliminated the fine print that includes cable and air-conditioning in your office, it might fall more in line with allocations. (Air conditioning in *Hell?* WHAT WERE YOU THINKING?!)

But that's not why I think your IQ is adrift in outer darkness. It's your utter failure to grasp the concept that you will *never* throttle the windpipes of this contemptible couple unless you orchestrate a precipitous drop in the performance of Organizational basics. These vile amphibians have an offensive array of daily, weekly, and monthly rituals that define them as "Saints"—meeting attendance, prayer, scriptures, tithing, fasting, Family Home Evening, temple attendance, etc., and so on, et al., *ad nauseam*. Until you undermine each and every one of these particulars, you're simply spinning your wheels. Better they are prompted to muse the mysteries of eternal life. Let them excogitate until doomsday the various riddles regarding Kolob and Kokaubeam while ignoring the more formidable foundations of the Archenemy's so-called plan. These despicable habits create a firewall around a family that shields them from our most aggressive assaults, entirely obstructing our ability to unleash carnage.

Do you realize that their attendance at Sabbath services was flawless last quarter? Obviously the only poltroon still snoozing Sunday morning is *you!* When their sacrament meeting rotated into the 8:00 a.m. timeslot, I felt certain you'd score a resounding victory. We snagged eight other families within their ward boundaries with this minor adjustment! Don't you get it? Discombobulate this habit for a few short weeks and—*presto change-o!*—we'll lure them into the quagmire of utter inactivity. It's a scream how easily such a modest transition can be exploited.

I'm also disturbed by your Target's continued dedication to twice-daily supplication, i.e., *prayer*. We've done precious little since his mission to stop these droll soliloquies to the Archenemy while he is bent on his knees. Yes, we *have*, on occasion, diminished a prayer's duration and intensity, but this is thoroughly inadequate. Keep whacking away! Such occurrences must be reduced by 50% before our next review or the Head Office has threatened to cancel our subscription to Diabolical Digest—just a month before I'm again slated to be featured on the cover!

The couple's consistency for daily scripture study is equally abhorrent. *Squelch it!* Do you hear me? Such practices are no less detestable than prayer. The hazards of the Archenemy's so-called "Holy Writ" are evident not only within the poisonous words themselves, but ensconced in the daily discipline of burying one's nose in its pages. Do you understand my meaning? Just a Target's *proximity* to these chapters and verses makes his spirit more accessible to raw revelation. Every time he inhales this propaganda, he becomes ensnared more securely inside the Archenemy's chamber of delirium—coaxed into an intoxicating communion with the eternal nature he aspires to emulate. Even a random sentence he memorized as a child will strike different chords with each subsequent phase of his life, revealing increasingly alarming insights.

We fear it less, of course, whenever only superficial meanings penetrate his mind, as when he tries to assimilate the monotonous harangues of that oh-so-grandiloquent prognosticator, Isaiah. It's only as Mr. Hansen learns the elusive art of *listening* that a kind of floodgate is opened and our warriors are swept desperately downstream. The best way to hinder this is by hiding the scriptures far beneath the bed, but if he somehow sneaks them past you and starts reading, let him be more attentive to quota than serious reflection.

If the goal, for instance, is to devour a single chapter each night, alter it to become a race against the clock. He should be thrilled if he tops his former record of consuming an entire page in 5.9 seconds. If his goal is associated directly with time—twenty minutes, for example—you must pester him with an unending parade of distractions, such as an unflossed particle of pork chop in his teeth. He'll move heedlessly from verse to verse without grasping a single phrase. Nevertheless, whisper into his ear, "What's the point of re-reading? After all, twenty minutes have lapsed. My goal has been met!"

Fasting is another repulsive pastime. To our relief, the actual incidence of this practice has dropped off substantially since your Target's two-year hiatus in Redneck-ville, USA. When the requisite week of fasting arrives, he usually fails to make note of it, reminded only as he sits in the pews and a breadline of testimony bearers make their way to the podium. Oh, he'll sometimes skip a meal in some half-baked attempt, but his heart is not really honed in to the cause. Casual fasts are priceless to observe.

Another alternative is to promote excessive zealousness, such as fasting for three days, coupled with subtle (or not-so-subtle) bluster and exaggerations of suffering. Like the Pharisees of old Jerusalem, we revel in the nullification of any sacrifice engendered by pride or self-aggrandizement.

With regard to temple attendance, I am so concerned and disappointed that I purchased a Kewpie doll in your image which I may torment and vex at my leisure. My records show that your Target attended twice in his first six months of marriage, while his wife went on three occasions. Although this is still well below the Organization's minimum recommendation (most shameful, perhaps, since they live only ten minutes away), it remains an obtrusive pimple on your department record. Get it through your skull! We cannot condone *any* attendance at that edifice! (Unless, of course, the Target attends *unworthily*, but that's another matter.)

A temple remains that single sanctum on earth where we cannot continually beleaguer and harass him. Often after he emerges he is *still* unapproachable for a period of time. At minimum, Frogknot, encourage conflicts in their schedule that will keep them from attending, especially as a couple. There are presently only a small number of spiritual activities beyond sacrament meeting that they practice together—and we wish to preserve that reality. Spiritual progression is always a frightening thing, but it's always better if it remains a solitary activity. We often hoodwink many married souls into believing that exaltation can be a self-centered enterprise, forgetting that real estate in the Celestial Kingdom must be purchased with *two* signatures.

Finally, why are these trilobites paying a full tithing? Your Target is only working part time. He *knows* he can hardly pay his monthly bills as it is! Can you at least manipulate him to tithe on the net rather than the gross? Can you help him to adopt the disposition that whatever he pays places heaven in his debt and that the Archenemy now owes him interest? We love to ravage these creatures' perceptions of gratitude whenever and wherever possible. My fear, Frogknot, is that you've allowed this practice to endure for so long now that he may be petrified of *not* paying his tithing, fully cognizant of the opportunities and blessings that he places at risk. Some of them fancy calling it "fire insurance," did you know that? Fire insurance, my eye! Wait'll I have him smoldering like a marshmallow on my stick!

I'd elaborate further on the extermination of gospel basics, but until your senses return from their prolonged sabbatical, such an outpouring of intelligence might cause you serious injury. Cripple each of the core components of faith that I've described or mark my words, Frogknot, that smoldering s'more will be *you*.

Your Capricious Counselor,
MUCKWHIP

28

From: "Muckwhip" <muckwhip@waydownbelow.hel>
To: <frogknot@waydownbelow.hel>
Subject: Subject: bumps in the road

MY DEAR FROGKNOT,

At last we have high hopes for lasting, mouth-watering progress. Good thing, too, since I was about to cancel your tee time at the club. Perhaps you weren't aware that you owned such a membership. Well, since we cannot currently condone recreation for our imps, I hardly thought it worth mentioning. But hey, I often acquire generous gifts for my fiends without actually informing them. It's just the kind of guy I am.

Less than a year into their marriage and already these two love-locusts have entangled themselves in an issue with no clear resolution. Or rather, not without capitulation on the part of one spouse or the other. These are always my favorite controversies. Why? Because there's never a real winner! Even if a victor is declared, the resentment left percolating just beneath the surface will always gestate to offer us fertile opportunities for the future.

You are to be commended for prompting Mr. Hansen to utter exactly the right phrases to inspire the loftiest levels of acrimony. However, don't think that just because wifie-poo has returned home to mummy and duddy that she accepts this as any kind of permanent solution. Too much has changed in her personality and in her parent's circumstances to allow her to procure the peace and security that she seeks. These accommodations, if she remains much longer, will only make her *more* disposed to reconcile. Even now she is realizing that her parents are no more likely to offer insight or clarification than anyone else. For once, there's no precedent. She's on her own. Not a happy realization, I assure you. What she will find most irritating is her parents' encouragement to accede to her husband's wishes, despite any personal devotion to their "little girl." But it's not *Mrs.* Hansen's feelings of betrayal that will benefit us most. It's those of her husband.

Your Target's perceptions of masculine authority are set in stone. In his opinion, the many years of savings his bride brought into the marriage should be used to their combined benefit, which in this case means that he can divert such capital to further his career ambitions. After all, didn't she agree that he could use these funds for such a purpose during their engagement? Of course, *her* interpretation was always that it would be spent on education—not squandered on bills and rent while he pursued his dream to become a professional musician.

This is a delicious conflict, Frogknot, and one which leaves us with so many promising strategies that it's hard to know where first to pounce. Fortunately for us, we have the benefit of pre-mortal hindsight.

We know, for instance, that Mr. Hansen does *not* possess the talent or temperament to succeed in such a competitive field as music performance. This is not wishful thinking on our part. We know it. We still recall the vast spectrum of pre-mortal history and it just isn't in him. No matter. We heartily *encourage* ambitions propelled by vanity—so long as they do not construct stronger "character." They must lead to inescapable despair. For reasons that we can only speculate, the Archenemy did not impart this gift to Mr. Hansen with the same liberality that He imparted it to others. Your job is to camouflage his true callings and capabilities as long as possible. By then we hope he is so peeved at the Archenemy—and by correlation, his own wife—that we may ignite the fuse for some intensely chromatic fireworks.

I find it hilarious when these creatures are given aspirations and inclinations without ability. Your Target will beat himself senseless against a concrete wall, and *still* find himself light-years from success. A shame really, knowing how easy it is to subvert and corrupt musicians. Artists can almost always be seduced into believing their powers of creativity place them above reproach when it comes to the ordinary rules of conduct that constrain mere mortals.

But never mind this. Your job is to keep him playing out this vainglorious charade down to the last red cent. Honestly, I doubt there's much that anyone could do to stop him. Heaven allows these creatures to pursue whatever floats their boats. Yes, it's that imbecilic free agency thing again. To our eternal annoyance, it's often in their failures that they find the grit to thwart us on subsequent battlefronts. So in this instance we'll focus principally on the impact that such pauperizing misadventures will have upon his marriage.

I know you placed a wager in the office pool, confident she would never capitulate to his perspective. I don't find fault with your intent, Frogknot. We *all* might have enjoyed listening to him howl the words that she "never really believed in or supported" him, laying all his disappointments and rejections squarely at her feet. But picture this, my myopic fiend—What if: (a) she gives in to him (grudgingly, of course), (b) he proceeds to blow all of their savings, as predicted, and (c) he blames her for his failure *anyway?!* Do you catch the vision? Do you perceive the potential? Oh, my midget-minded imp—this is going to be *exquisite!* Sorry that you will lose your wager. But I've never condoned office gambling anyway, unless all the odds are with the House. The House being me.

Your Target already knows that his spouse disapproves of his choices. Her background of poverty has given her a mindset which is much more practical on finances. She tends to resist the unfamiliar. No surprise here. For many females *security* is the thing that propels them to marriage in the first place. For men, it's, well . . . that *other* thing, first and foremost, but that's a different conversation. Be assured that the tempters who have charge over his wife will encourage her to let slip a multitude of sighs, rolls of the eyes, and verbal expressions of fear and doubt. Help him to make note of every single one. He must tally them up on a non-erasable mental list. Thus, when the day of defeat finally dawns, he'll irreversibly conclude that it was her lack of belief that, in the end, kept him from believing in himself.

Do not forget that our overriding goal is to capsize this marriage. Not merely to afflict it with unhappiness. Or even to let it slog along with mutual indifference. You must *terminate* it. This is defined by one word—divorce. The crumbling of covenants. The extirpation of promises. Nothing less will do.

Our ablest allies in marital demolition are always selfishness, misunderstanding, grudge-holding, mistrust, and pride. But selfishness remains my personal favorite. The Archenemy wants this duo to become an *uno*. Selfishness ensures that this can never happen. It keeps a marriage perpetually engulfed in a contest for *control*. Keep them relentlessly campaigning to either seize it or preserve it. Fortunately for us, we're presiding over two determinedly self-willed souls. Neither will freely concede without a fight. For now the conflict is financial, but additional categories will likewise prove entertaining. Intimacy, for example. But I'll discuss that subject at length in another h-mail.

Until then, endeavor to underscore any attempt at reconciliation with as much resentment and ill-will as the circumstances allow. Something was definitely lost in this latest conflict. Of course, we know it was only innocence. The veil of bliss that so assuredly enshrouds these oh-so-naïve newlyweds has finally dissipated. But to them, let it be an erosion of faith in the institution of marriage itself, and an affirmation that this whole thing might just turn out to be not nearly as fun as it was first envisioned. In short, not at all like the brochure.

Your Optimistic Oppressor,
MUCKWHIP

29

From: "Muckwhip" <muckwhip@waydownbelow.hel>

To: <frogknot@waydownbelow.hel>

Subject: bumps of a different sort

MY DEAR FROGKNOT,

I realize that until now I've been terribly remiss to give you the kudos you think you so deeply deserve. Even now my index finger hovers above the phone, just twitching to contact the Head Office and sing your praises. Unfortunately, I stubbed the appendage recently whilst scratching my infraorbital furrow. As I'm sure you understand, I cannot aggravate the injury. Perhaps next month, my fretful fiend.

Until then, it looks like you have an *overabundance* of material at your disposal. I must say, the timing of his wife's announcement that the litmus on the pregnancy strip indicated a + instead of a – appears no less than devil-sent. (Okay, "devil-sent" may be a stretch since we are presently unable to replicate the powers of reproduction. All of our experiments to fabricate a tabernacle of flesh have thus far been less than successful, calling into question the myth of a million-and-one uses for duct tape and chewing gum. No matter. Our experts at R&D are actively pursuing promising alternatives. I understand scrapbooking supplies and a hot glue gun are under investigation.)

Still, considering the drama this announcement will ignite, it's sometimes hard to believe the Opposition isn't working secretly for *us*. Not surprisingly, Mr. Hansen's efforts to chalk up any success as a musician have remained elusive. His reaction to his wife's news was, as we clearly foresaw, panic and incredulity combined with an audible gulp. Your added touch of wheedling him to accentuate his faux pas with several nonsensical expostulations was priceless. And at such an ill-timed moment! She'll store these boneheaded phrases in her memory bank much like a squirrel stockpiles acorns—and if she blinks, we'll regale her with persistent reminders. Did he really imply that *she* may be culpable for the failure of their contraceptives? Ah, so typical of a male. Still, I never cease to be amused. I must also compliment you for persuading him several months ago that they could not possibly afford health insurance. Insult to injury is a resplendent thing, and since these grunions seem incapable of perceiving any future beyond their current moment of misery, it should greatly enhance the home's atmosphere of oppressive claustrophobia. And not a twinkle too soon, I might add.

I've noticed that ever since his wife returned to her mommy and daddy, Mr. Hansen was honestly evaluating her opinion on matters of economy and *esprit de corps* far too often. I'd even noted that he *once* (yes, I realize it was a rare instance) acquiesced to her point of view! It was completely vulgar and obscene! He was obviously breathing in too many paint fumes! And nothing could have been more nauseating than all the cooing and purring that transpired after they settled their argument.

You must be relentlessly vigilant, Frogknot. Such a disposition could become more beneficial to the Archenemy's objectives than it first appears. He absolutely relishes any developments that might encourage your Target to devote more attention to his family. Actually, He prefers it whenever your Target focuses on *any* interests outside himself. Don't be outfoxed by the Archenemy's wiles. He deceives us time and again by mingling with every adversity an advantageous and unexpected outcome. Not here, Frogknot. Not now. Your Target's sentiments that he is being forced to sacrifice his dreams in favor of financial security must remain a tenacious source of disappointment. Let the blame be ever directed toward his wife, his tadpoles, and ultimately, his God.

We fear he'll now accept the job offer that his father presented a few months back to enter the family heating and air conditioning business. Your Target, as we both know, has always felt this vocation was beneath him. Therefore he'll likely view it as a temporary diversion. As a result, he'll avoid every opportunity that the profession provides for training and advancement. The timing could not be better to infect this marriage with as much turmoil, bickering, and intolerance as the circumstances permit. His patience must have an eternally short fuse. If possible, provide him with many occasions wherein he will express heartfelt dissatisfaction to friends. Not *real* friends, mind you. But yes-men who are ever sympathetic and supportive of his flaws. Chances are, many of them will possess similar shortcomings. The maxim still holds that misery loves company. Eventually, and for obvious reasons, I propose that some of those sympathetic ears be female.

A certain consequence of his spouse's pregnancy for the next few months hasn't even been discussed—that of her marked loss of interest in certain activities for which the Target's interests haven't changed. He has already discovered, to his complete surprise, that his own needs and those of his wife are not always equal. They are driven by various and alternating stimuli. Still, *nothing* has prepared him for the frustrations that await.

You must inflame an awful possibility inside him, Frogknot—a trembling terror that matters of intimacy between himself and his bride will never again be the same. Undoubtedly some features of their relationship have already lost a certain novelty. If we have been successful at all in engendering within him the corrupted attitudes of his culture, it is *variety* and *novelty* that he should find most mysterious and intriguing. Thus, you must now expand his appetite for such unfulfilled needs. The media will aid you enormously here, forever advertising the notion that he might be missing out on something extraordinary—something his present circumstances will never provide. "Never" is a very lonely word to individuals who are implacably addicted to novelty. It has an echoing effect that continually increases in amplitude and allurement.

Frame before your Target's imagination the folk figure of a man—a hero on horseback, rifle at the ready, who rides into town, righting wrongs and vanquishing the most beleaguering *bandoleros*—all before the watchful eyes of swooning lasses. Here is a man who loves remorselessly until, alas, he must ride on into the sunset of his next adventure. Such a swashbuckler will never settle down. His passion is for adventure and exploration, not commitment. There is certainly no time for family or fatherhood. We cloak such visions behind the poetic banner of sucking the marrow out of life and savoring every flavor and spice the world can furnish. We know perfectly well that the ones we seduce with such drivel are *never* satisfied and are forever searching, but this is precisely the lamp we want your pestiferous insect fluttering and flapping against for his entire existence.

For now, emphasize the mundane, routine, and repetitive nature of his present circumstances. If your Target is the restless, self-centered rogue that I know he can be, we'll have him riding off into the sunset and straight over a cliff in no time flat. And the trophy, Frogknot, will be all yours—provided, of course, that you can furnish the shelf space it so rightfully deserves. If such accoutrements are lacking, I'll humbly accept the honor on your behalf and exhibit it for safe keeping among my own accolades.

Your Unassuming Executive,
MUCKWHIP

30

From: "Muckwhip" <muckwhip@waydownbelow.hel>
To: <frogknot@waydownbelow.hel>
Subject: arrival

MY DEAR FROGKNOT,

Hopscotching down the yellow brick road of sentimentality, is he? Given to fits of blathering incoherences like "awhhhhhh" and "coochy-coo?"

Unfortunately, this is more commonly a transitory psychosis. Every newly ordained nincompoop known as a "father" becomes effectively inebriated with saccharine-laced schmaltz whenever another of those slimy, hairless bundles of corporeal corruption slithers from the womb and sucks its first breath of putrefied air. While he remains in this state, I fear you'll find it difficult to make any practical progress. Ah, but wait! A few nights of this creature's colicky conniptions is a sure antidote to all of Mr. Hansen's fantasies of what he was about to inherit. And from everything that we already know about this bitsy anklebiter (that is, from our associations with him in the pre-mortal realm), we're confident that he'll be as boisterous as they come.

The miniature twit. The traitor. I'll never understand the Archenemy's rationale for dilly-dallying so long before allowing the birth of malevolent little reprobates like *him*. More and more of the most aggravating spirits with whom we grappled in the War in Heaven are making their earthly debut. It occurs almost hourly. Where in Hell's half-acre are they all coming from? I loathe every driblet of their germ-ridden spittle! Do you realize what this whimpering, squirting, excreting ragamuffin could *do* for this family? He could bring them *joy!* Intolerable, insufferable joy! We'll have *none* of it! No! Not allowed! Not by the hair of my chin, nostrils, or earlobes! The very notion crawls up my craw and afflicts me with unremitting heebie-jeebies. Rest assured we'll assign fiends who will orchestrate this whippersnapper's total destruction. According to the Archenemy's obnoxious rules, he may not be held to account for eight long years. Nevertheless, there remain umpteen objectives we can still achieve in the interim to train him on the utmost advantages of all-out anarchy and bedlam.

Of course, your Target and his wife remain our principal focal points in preventing this pollywog from ever realizing anything remotely comparable to his foreordained destiny. Therefore, you must step up your efforts against Mr. Hansen with indefatigable ferocity. The rewards of perpetuating a divorce after the introduction of offspring are indelibly toothsome—all the more tasty every time the total number of toddlers in the quiver accrues. We'll welcome victory in this category however we can tally it. So don't ever doubt that there will come a better time or opportunity than now.

You write in your latest dispatch that the bitterness your Target sustains after being forced to abandon his music career still gurgles and simmers beneath the surface. Well, if that's as true as you say, tell me *why has he returned to school* to become certified in his present occupation!? In my opinion, he looks more to be settling in. This is despicable, Frogknot. You must keep the carrot of dissatisfaction dangling perpetually before his nostrils. Can you coerce him to cross paths with other musicians, particularly those of close acquaintance—men and women who are plying the trade with an obvious degree of success? The goal is to stir up jealousies and resentments whose chains he'll never escape. If I may broach a suggestion, why not impel him to answer a call to the abode of a successful local musician in order to suck lint out of his heating duct? *That's* the kind of humiliation I'm talking about! For pity's sake, Frogknot, dredge up some imagination!

Did you think it would please me to learn that he is taking on guitar students or accepting invitations to perform in smaller venues? Think again, you numskull! Unless these events can be twisted to foster a more gargantuan need for the spotlight, it offers us no momentum for progress. Don't you get it, Frogknot? He must DESPISE his life! This loathing is only kept alive by continually feeding his restlessness and vanity. Do you grasp what the Archenemy is trying to do here? Let me clarify in case your feeble mind has failed to comprehend. He's convincing your Target to orient his priorities!

Mr. Hansen would certainly be shocked to the core to learn that the Opposition is far more inclined toward saving his soul than salvaging his musical aspirations. Thus, it's imperative that we keep his priorities forever knotted and tangled into impossible snarls. Every failure experienced by our department in our effort to reverse the order of God, family, career, and leisure always lurches back to bite us in the posterior. But in the case of males, ever scraping and clawing for greater status in the pride, it's invariably advantageous to pervert his emphasis on career.

Just for fun, I'll mention another arena wherein we'd like you to begin meddling. Until this day your Target has had his "significant other" all to himself. He must now begin to feel particularly "put out" to be tussling and competing for his wife's attention. It will only hit him by degrees just how much his desires and routines have been shanghaied by the stork's latest parcel. No more spontaneous getaways, fewer extemporaneous exploits, and best of all, the realization that every destination must now be accompanied by an increasingly heavy, high-maintenance pest. All of this should naturally chafe your Target's disposition, but it's up to you to embolden him to express this disgruntlement in a way that adds the greatest degree of marital friction.

Again, matters of intimacy should become your fundamental point of attack. The male of the species can be profoundly selfish when it comes to this preoccupation. You must provoke your Target to see romance much the same way he views his cravings for a medium-rare rib-eye. He hungers, therefore he must feast. He thirsts, therefore he must drink. The family's new addition will aid us tremendously. Its very presence will frequently postpone passions and interrupt innumerable romantic escapades, obliterating both of its parent's expectations. This is where the battle of the sexes really heats up, becoming uncompromisingly merciless. If we play it right, both parties will decide it's patently hopeless to achieve any state of unity or happiness while the other exists in the same solar system.

So go ahead and bask in the glow of your wriggling newborn, Mr. Hansen! Let yourself be incurably smitten by its first smile or amused to the point of apoplexy when it spits up on your shoulder. Your humor will wear thinner and thinner over time. I guarantee it.

But for the time being, Frogknot, you may want to invest in a snug pair of earmuffs. All the hoopla and celebration from the Archenemy's ranks as they cheer their newest arrival are causing me a throbbing migraine.

Your Suffering CEO,
MUCKWHIP

31

MY DEAR FROGKNOT,

You're making me inordinately dizzy, my apprentice. One week with your Target and his wife it's pouting and pettiness and the next week it's forgiveness and felicity. This is no way to operate a marriage. Either the parties are spiraling out of control or they are elevating toward the celestial happy-hunting grounds. No more of this make-up, chrysanthemums-and-chocolates, kissy-kissy gobbledygook and falderal. Their family cabinet should be disproportionately stocked with grudge pudding, sour grapes, and short fuses. Every conflict—even if temporarily assuaged—must leave behind some noxious reminder, like a bereft rodent in the ventilation. Over time the scent and sentiment must become insufferable.

To accomplish this you must ratchet up the bickering, especially over frivolous minutia. We in Hell adore bickering and contention. No symphony is more mellifluous. I myself have box seats at every significant global conflict. Don't deny yourself such indulgences, Frogknot, even in your lowly assignment. Conduct your own orchestra of acrimony in the

Hansen household. I'd like to think that your Target has far more complaints regarding his spouse than those he has previously stated. So—*why isn't he restating them?!* Re-emphasizing? Re-exhorting? He should be fuming, sputtering, seething, and exuding the most virulent marital venom. Certainly the home in which he was reared has provided copious examples for him to emulate. Mr. Hansen is displaying a disgraceful lack of commitment to carrying on this tradition to the next generation. Shouldn't your Target be repeatedly comparing his wife to his mother? (Not that his mother was always such a pillar of perfection, but for our present needs please perpetuate this myth.) He should be articulating and emblazoning his spouse's shortcomings on an hourly basis!

For instance, I'm quite certain they both learned very different habits and routines about child-rearing. Such roof-raising disputations should be among your most cherished pastimes, and if possible, they should always take place in front of the child. Inject into all their personal behaviors a corrosive lack of discipline when it comes to muzzling their tempers in the presence of progeny. Arguments are never as entertaining and *advantageous* for us when all the fireworks are suppressed until they can be discharged in a setting of relative privacy. Spontaneous combustions of bickering help us enormously to educate a child in the ways of contention. Later on such undisciplined behavior teaches the scions to pit both parents against each other at opportune junctures and elevate the mercury on all family squabbles.

However, Frogknot, if you haven't realized, it's often *not* the most glaring flaws that obliterate a marriage. It's those thousand-and-one nit-picky irks. With a modicum of finesse on our part, even the most paltry irritations can end up rubbing the most sensitive surfaces raw—especially if the other partner views them as deliberate and premeditated. Now is your chance to grind in the salt, especially since the birth of their second sniveler—a girl this time—leaves both parents vulnerable to the inflammatory symptoms of exhaustion. It's when they are overwrought that we have so much success encouraging them to argue over *arguments*—who started them, why, who bears blame, who made the initial affront, etc. They don't even need to remember what set off the conflict! The conversation invariably digresses into a futile dissection of intent, tone-of-voice, semantics, and insensitivity. The whole scene is tremendously entertaining!

I'd also like you to take better advantage of your Target's stereotypes regarding gender roles. We've been planting detonation devices all the way back to his infancy in hopes of one day setting off an incomparable conflagration. Remember to depress the plunger well before his bride, bishop or any other meddling provocateurs have an opportunity to enlighten him.

Keep your Target reluctant to perform common household and child care chores. Smuggle into his mind the rationale that after a hard day's work he deserves a well-earned break, and that dishes and diapers are feminine responsibilities. In time we hope to have his wife veritably yanking out her follicles as she wonders when *her* respite might materialize, which, if we have any say, is never. I'll ensure that the tempters in charge of Mrs. Hansen make her complaints as frenetic and hyperventilated as possible to incite your Target's natural defense mechanisms and guarantee a lack of empathy. His wife's team leader, Weedpuss, is also looking to introduce yet another tactic into his wide-ranging repertoire—that of withholding affection from her spouse unless he enthusiastically assents to her demands. Mr. Hansen is certain to be pathetically unprepared against such stratagems, although each incidence will fertilize a fresh layer of rancor.

So either *derail* this roller coaster, Frogknot, or give me *Dramamine!* It's all the interminable dips and climbs that I can no longer stomach. In the first phase of marriage such ups and downs too often imply a steady ascent. Send this barrel plummeting over the falls! Let this family drown in its own audacity for thinking they could possibly construct something eternal in the face of devils of our intestinal fortitude. *Preposterous!*

Now if you'll excuse me, I'm waxing a bit woozy. There's a brouhaha in the bakery. Or in other words, I'm about to toss my cookies.

Your Hurling Hegemon,
MUCKWHIP

32

From: "Muckwhip" <muckwhip@waydownbelow.hel>
To: <frogknot@waydownbelow.hel>
Subject: upsetting practices

MY DEAR FROGKNOT,

I infer from your last communiqué that you are of the conviction that we may be sadly lacking in effective work incentives. Therefore I am now offering an all-expense paid vacation to Nott Berry Fun—Hell's recently inaugurated amusement park. Sort of a devil's answer to Disneyland. As of yet there are no attractions, but plenty of lines.

However, Frogknot, if you hope to qualify for the drawing, you had better frustrate a few more of the gospel fundamentals that still dominate your Target's daily and weekly routine. Again, stop those infuriating prayers! With just a minute amount of additional faith and fervency from Mr. Hansen such monologues could easily become *dialogues!* Don't you *dare* let it go that far! You must also earnestly lessen any instances of *family* prayer—unless of course you *welcome* the inconvenience of battling through impenetrable barricades and forbidding force fields in your attempts to infiltrate the premises!

Thankfully, there remain a few favorable chinks in their defenses. Recurrent apathy and breakfast-time pandemonium have allowed us to at least massacre any commitment to keep up the ritual of *morning* prayer. Furthermore, his wife's team of tempters deserves credit for convincing her that such supplications should not be engaged while in the midst of marital quibbling, thus assisting us in prolonging such tensions *ad infinitum.* Nevertheless, I insist that you can still do better. I spit and fume to see his spouse kneeling every night with those obnoxious little aphids. It's brainwashing, pure and simple! As you may recall from Temptation 101, few prayers are more strangulating to our enterprises than those muttered by moppets. A child's supplications must be muzzled at any cost! Seldom will a child pray without persistent nagging from Mommy and Daddy. Thus—attack the parents! Afflict them with interruption, disturbance, apathy and distraction.

You noted that your Target has announced renewed commitment to the practice of Family Home Evening. Normally I would not oppose your strategy of modulating this effort into an exercise in utter futility—plagued by rambunctiousness and sedition—but the down and dirty of it is that this ceremony cannot be condoned in *any* form. You see, the Archenemy's earthly representatives—those treacherous prophets and apostles—have gone and imbued the whole proceeding with some terribly toxic promises. They've proclaimed that its faithful performance each and every Monday night effectuates the warranty that *all* of their urchins—even those who backslide—will eventually circumambulate back to the flock. Can you conceive such absurdity? We have no *antidote* for such a bombastic proclamation! Just another of the Opposition's excessively unfair policies.

Yet despite the boldness of this warranty, we still find the practice surprisingly simple to repress. Repeat to your Target that his unruly whippersnappers are still too wet behind the ears. They already possess the attention spans of ferrets. Only if his wife persists are you instructed to pursue your original course of uninterrupted mayhem. Hopefully Mrs. Honey-pie will quickly decide that her husband's commitment to the cause is dreadfully lacking, and thus feel overwhelmingly discouraged.

I'm no less agitated to hear that your Target has accepted his bishop's invitation to become a Primary instructor. What tomfoolery is this? Why did you not nudge him to profess that he has advanced oh-so-far beyond such menial assignments? Why didn't you shout into his ear that his schedule contains irreconcilable conflicts? Why didn't you *scream* into his psyche that he couldn't possibly give to the calling the time that such a sacred duty deserves? Or—as remains one of my perennial favorites—that it's simply not a proper application of his copious talents? Or that his earlobes temperamentally twitch when tossed into a lion's den of toddlers? Great gads, there are an *infinite* number of excuses! *Pick* one!

It would be a hoot if he could assert that his bishop suffers a deficiency of inspiration. Our objective is to make sure that even the most worthy ward members are oppressively overtaxed. Four or five callings at *minimum!* The Organization should remain universally understaffed, drawing even the most valiant into full inactivity. (And if we're even luckier, taxied off in a padded truck!)

Lately we've found it amusing to enlist a sort of glorified game of cat-and-mouse. Presently the Organization seems to place more emphasis on family activities rather than chores for the Church. So our strategy is now to persuade a Target to neglect religious duty in favor of *anything* that keeps him home, such as that not-to-be-missed episode of American Beach Boxing Bimbos. Not long ago we encouraged just the opposite, convincing religious enthusiasts to feel justified in neglecting family duties in favor of service to higher purposes.

Since our preference is always the extreme over moderation, we must adjust our game plan accordingly. If all else fails, you must render his service to the Organization ineffectual. We in

Hell *adore* long-winded meetings, always preferring yak-yak-yakking over practical action. Frequent and overlong sit-downs do much to salve the conscience of interminably lazy Saints. Of course, we wouldn't object to the notion of *no* meetings either. Again, extremism good; moderation bad.

I'm additionally concerned with his revitalized interest in home teaching. Our goal has always been to transmogrify this enterprise into a certifiably negative pastime. Even when a Target bites the bullet and ambles up the walkway to his assignee's doorbell, he must never contribute any measurable obstruction to whatever pestilential operations we are undertaking in that home. Conversation must be kept trivial and inconsequential. The event itself must remain void of preparation, planning, or prayer. This will keep the recipients of such visits oblivious, and even resistant to these intruders, viewing the experience not as an enterprise that fosters camaraderie, but as an uncomfortable interruption to be endured with antsy fidgets and tight smiles.

For the most part the Organization has long been embarrassingly ineffective in this pursuit, especially among the priesthood. We are far more concerned by the persistent efforts of the sisters (those so-called "visiting teachers"). Here our objective is generally to transform their visits into gossip-fests that successfully reinforce coteries and cliques. It is rare that anyone actually goes the "extra mile." Easy enough to inveigle them to avoid the extra *yard!*

How soon these Saints seem to forget that the Organization's success or failure rests entirely upon the worker ants. Fortunately for us, the cumulative effect of a people once blessed, when they begin to forgo the farm, is that we gain supplemental powers that we would have otherwise not obtained. It's the little battles, like yours, that assure our perpetual supremacy.

If you can just undermine his *prayers*, Frogknot, I'll happily enter your name in the drawing for a well-deserved convalescence. I'll also ignore that teensy setback last week when Mr. and Mrs. Hansen consented to marriage counseling. Wasn't it you who assured me beyond all ambiguity that your Target was far too proud to submit to such lunacy? Oh well. I suspect his wife only intends to make the appointment a gripe session, her finger sharply pointed at her spouse with the primal, almost canine-esque command to "Fix!" We fully expect lawyers to arrive on scene by year's end. Now there's a gala that should earn Gehenna's engrossed attention! Tickets will be reserved only for Hell's most eminent dignitaries.

Your Resilient Ringmaster,
MUCKWHIP

33

From: "Muckwhip" <muckwhip@waydownbelow.hel>
To: <frogknot@waydownbelow.hel>
Subject: yes!

MY DEAR FROGKNOT,

She did it! She used the "D" word! I am quite literally beaming with pride! I am veritably glowing with puckish satisfaction. I should attach a photo of myself, acknowledging the infrequency of such a condition. My coordinated efforts with both teams in charge of your Target and Mrs. Hansen are at long last beginning to pay off—and *generously!* I feel like a parent watching his little niblet pop his first home run. If I had cigars, I'd distribute them liberally amongst all fiends involved.

With the "D" word now drizzled sumptuously upon the concoction, we find ourselves armed to the teeth with fresh munitions to utterly annihilate this marriage. The word itself opens up a kind of magical gateway that allows a dramatic acceleration of all our efforts. Just the verbalization of "divorce" forces these fungi to seriously excogitate the option, ruminate the ramifications, and visualize a tantalizing fantasy of what their world might be like without the other mega-mutant around to muck it up. They may find the initial visions disturbing and scary, but never mind. They'll acclimatize to the idea soon enough. In the meantime, you must increase your insurgency with renewed and unprecedented energy.

In case you haven't observed it for yourself, their eldest son is mature enough to gauge the complexities behind most of their quarrels. This will aid in our plan to eviscerate the lad's self-confidence and inner security. Even your Target's eldest daughter is perceptive of the situation. Their second daughter is too young at the moment to be visibly perturbed, however . . . I must admit, Frogknot, this damsel #2 causes me far more anxiety than the other children combined. I can't put my finger on it. Perhaps it's merely that I know her so well from our unhappy associations in the pre-mortal realm, but . . . No, it's something else. I'll figure it out. And when I do, we'll bring to bear every necessary weapon.

Above all else, steer your Target and his wife far afield of bishops or stake presidents. These people, even if they prove the most inept marriage counselors, wield a spiritual mantle of an unparalleled sophistication when it comes to calling forth the fury and might of the Archenemy. The last thing we need is interference from their bumbling bishop.

I note with some disappointment your emasculating failure at motivating your Target to bring out-and-out pornography into his domicile. There exists such an abundance of opportunities now that you have no sensible excuse. Your achievements are a disgrace to those of us who have worked tirelessly for so many decades to saturate popular entertainment with such a bountiful variety of filth and pestilence.

I suppose I am marginally appeased by the fact that your Target and his wife recently attended several movies with a controversial MPAA rating. Their excuse—which I love every time I hear it—was that the flick was reviewed as having important cultural appeal, and was therefore exempt from usual prohibitions. As a result, you subjected them both to a full forty-five seconds of some of the steamiest pornography we've ever effectuated—and all in the noble cause of artistic expression. Because you managed to at least crack open the door, I fully expect your Target will lower the bar even further and eventually grant the term "cultural appeal" a much broader definition.

Try this bit of logic on him (it's my favorite of late, and surprisingly effective): Remind him that the holy scriptures themselves portray innumerable "R" and "X-rated" spectacles. Whisper, "Why, the world *itself* is R-rated! What I see on the screen only reflects that which I witness in real life." Now don't scoff, Frogknot. This methodology of whitewashing suits our purposes swimmingly. Rationalizations are, in fact, a dime a dozen, yet these earthworms seem increasingly willing to genuflect to whatever justification we have on hand.

Still, I can hardly be satisfied until you actually introduce these infections directly into their home. Without sin, our access to the Hansen household is effectively stonewalled. Granted, our imps have already managed an admirable level of access on account of marital contention, but imagine how effusively we could permeate the premises if we succeeded in introducing out-and-out sleeze! We'd cut door keys for every fiend in our department. Your Target's abode would become the most happenin' pad in the neighborhood.

Imagine yourself, Frogknot, the proud proprietor of one the most salacious saturnalias in all the Dominion of Discord. *All* of us would come to your party. I'd expedite invitations to some of our most prestigious tempters—including those engaged in the arts of physical and sexual abuse. And imagine, Frogknot—just imagine if at one of those balmy banquets you were honored by an impromptu appearance from the big boss himself? You think I exaggerate?? If you prevail in this campaign, it's entirely possible!

The means of conveyance for such slime is not especially important, whether it's photographs, broadcasts, DVDs, downloads, etc. We proudly provide a smorgasbord of smut! In his spouse's case, her tempters have successfully directed her toward some of our racier mass-market romances. Since a woman's faculties for stimulation are somewhat different from a man's—less visual and more emotional—we find this avenue of defilement considerably more advantageous.

And if I might offer another two cents, let me suggest that your Target take a tour of the tantalizing buffet we've made available on the World Wide Web. This clever little tool has allowed us to seduce even the most resistant souls—those who might otherwise have been stalwart soldiers in the forces of the Archenemy. These are the types who would never have been caught dead purchasing printed matter. And yet the convenience of the internet spears them like fish in a barrel. Our most brutal, addictive, and malignant masterpieces now lurk as effortlessly near as a few measly mouse clicks. Treasure the irony as your Target, suffering serious dejection from run-ins with his wife, hides himself in secret household nooks, fixed inescapably to the seductive allure of that incandescent computer screen.

If you can succeed in this single enterprise, Frogknot, Mr. Hansen will be yours. Break out the barbecue. Sharpen the silverware. You might even cajole him to strike up an acquaintance with some other lecherous lonely heart on the other side of the world, or maybe even just across town! A match made in Hell, if I do say so myself. And as long as you keep him separated from meddling bishops and other repentance-inducing stimuli, his attempts to escape will prove utterly in vain.

It's times like these that I truly envy you, Frogknot. *Nothing!*— not even the privileges of my current position—equals the sheer satisfaction of witnessing the relentless unraveling of eternal covenants. Let's just say such thoughts cause me to sigh with nostalgia.

Now look, I've gone and gotten all misty. I really am just a syrupy sentimentalist at heart.

Your Maudlin Maharajah,
MUCKWHIP

34

From: "Muckwhip" <muckwhip@waydownbelow.hel>
To: <frogknot@waydownbelow.hel>
Subject: in the groove

MY DEAR FROGKNOT,

Will your triumphs never cease? You're on a roll, my resplendent apprentice! The scent of divorce is in the air, like blood in the water or the thrashings of a wounded animal in the forest, drawing in hungry and merciless predators. Those predators are *us*, Frogknot, and our claws are assiduously stropped.

I must compliment you in particular for the one-two punch you orchestrated with Weedpuss, the team leader in charge of his wife. A victory parade is assured for both of you a soon as this onerous undertaking is concluded. I see it now!—your neon-pulsing float rolling forward just behind and below my own. Exercise your waving hand, my splendid subordinates!

I might have preferred it if he had indeed packed up and left his house by the weekend, according to his wife's demands. But the alternative of having *her* as the unhappy sot who takes the initiative of moving out has a certain sparkly appeal. My only fear is that having his wife and four whippersnappers move into the home of Mr. Hansen's sister bristles with too many prospects for an eventual reconciliation. Her tempters are powerfully advocating for her to pursue the notion of renting an apartment, especially if it has a minimum 12-month lease. The longer the prospect of marital separation, the less any likelihood of meaningful resolution.

In essence, they are engaged in a "practice divorce." This allows our Targets time to experience the full range of animosity, independence, bitterness, and disdain. Hearts will hardly grow fonder in such circumstances. Only colder. Thus, it becomes our job—nay, our sacred *duty!*—to repeatedly remind them both of past offenses, incurable flaws, and favorable prospects for the future—without that other wretch anywhere in the vicinity to louse it all up!

Place your target perpetually in the presence of those who have also tossed in the towel. Nothing soothes and acclimatizes the human consciousness toward the checkmate of divorce like a fellow divorcee. Remember his miserable friend from high school who devolved to become one of our bawdiest bachelors? Command your Target to dial his digits this instant!

As for other ongoing tactics, steady as she goes, Captain Frogknot. Hold firm to your present course. As long as Mr. Hansen feels he can lay claim to the "moral high ground," the more blinded he will remain to his own accountabilities. After all, *she* left *him*—not vice versa. Repeat this in his brain like a broken record. This will allow him to feel justified in abdicating the fight with a clear conscience, thus failing to recognize his own contribution to the disaster.

Divorce is unmistakably a blame game, and the essential object of your being is to prompt the Target to do . . . *nothing!* At least when it comes to contemplating reconciliation. Inaction resulting from pride and self-pity can be as deadly as a frontal assault with a phalanx of lances. In the event that your man concludes (correctly) that his wife's conduct is simply a desperate cry for attention and love, this too should be received by him with only a humdrum dismissal and grunt.

After all, to give in to her now will only encourage similar behavior in the future. Don't let it register quite yet that there *is* no future. For now let him think only of tomorrow and fantasize that she is teetering on the very precipice of full capitulation. For now just repeat that he is teaching this stubborn prima donna an essential lesson for her own good.

I'm also pleased that the current situation has induced both parties to practice only limited activity in the Organization. Didn't I tell you, Frognot? *Attrition: there is no substitute!* Remain relentless! This is your prime opportunity to cut off every breath of soul-saving oxygen that the Organization might pump into his lungs. But take careful heed. The Archenemy is certainly conjuring a few tricks of His own. One might be that not attending his meetings will raise a red flag to home teachers or other spiritual leaders. Normally this is not a concern, but stay on your toes. The passage of time and the inaccessibility of our subjects usually render interference from others inconsequential. My instincts tell me that this one is headed down in flames, another facsimile in the endless array of Sopwith Camels that I can etch along my fuselage.

After the divorce is finalized, I will have a lengthy to-do list for how you will deliver the remnants of Mr. Hansen's tattered soul into the hands of our infernal father. The last thing we desire is for a victory of this magnitude to morph into some sort of revival of religious sentiment. Incredible as it seems, the Archenemy is willing to succor even His most insipid hatchlings, so long as they slither back to him with broken spirits and contrite hearts. We'll entertain nothing of that sort on *my* watch. Am I to be called monstrously cruel for kicking a man while he's down?

I certainly hope so.

Your Callous Caliph,
MUCKWHIP

35

From: "Muckwhip" <muckwhip@waydownbelow.hel>
To: <frogknot@waydownbelow.hel>
Subject: not discouraged

MY DEAR FROGKNOT,

Look at that.

My typing fingers are much steadier than I might have expected considering the CATASTROPHIC developments so recently pronounced. Or maybe it's just that my innards are bloated with far too many incompetent tempters.

No, I don't think that's it. Curiously, the more I eat, the hungrier I become.

So Mrs. Hansen and her gruesome little hooligans are home again. Never mind. It remains my firm conviction that there is no measurable change in the underpinnings of this marriage. The motivations that brought this twosome back together all seem diametrically opposed to the Archenemy's prime directive, which is (prepare yet again to retch) that these two sniveling shrews become "one." I feel certain that your Target, despite the cheesy scene he performed on his sister's porch, fully intends to revert to his former routine of apathy, pouting, and self-indulgence—just as soon as he feels it's "safe." Keep in mind that his honey pie's change of heart may have hinged on the discovery that her pocketbook was bare. It appears she wasn't quite ready to live independent of her husband's income.

Unfortunately, a profound motivation for reconciling these tiffs is often rooted in the fear of how it may affect their tender-hearted bumpkins. This happens only if we fail to reinforce the fib that their eminently resilient rugrats will be just fine. Their eldest snot-wiper, now at the cusp of adolescence, has increasingly shown a commendable lack of interest in school and extra-curricular activities. The eldest lass in line has also focused her energies on *anything* that helps her to drift *away* from the family. Shortly we plan to vivify in her an exuberant, albeit premature, interest in lads, levity, and liquor.

The second eldest daughter still vexes me. Now approaching the age of accountability, it seems she has adopted the role of family peacemaker. Unfortunately, she's rather good at it. *Oh, I despise her, Frogknot!* I just wish I knew *why!* Why is my revulsion for her so deep and visceral?

Oh, well. She is the singular exception to our promising state of progress. Even ankle-biter number four has demonstrated ear-rending talent for toddler tantrums that ratchets up everyone's level of stress. Anxiety indubitably breeds egocentricity. It's a marvelous cycle. The next time the Hansen's are teetering on the brink of divorce, we will assuredly introduce the distortion that such a decision may actually be *better* for the children.

Although I scorn the motivations that brought these maudlin lovers back together, the Archenemy doesn't find their rationale for drawing back together nearly as repugnant as you might imagine. It's incomprehensible to us, but He often seems far less interested in the compatibility of personalities than in the *preservation of commitments*.

It pains me to admit that it is most often through *overcoming* life's piddling obstacles that the majority of these cantankerous couples are propelled toward that elusive state of "oneness" to which they originally aspired. The cement that seals their foreordained destiny is located within the fiber of commitment itself—ingrained in the molecules of endurance, tolerance, and long-suffering. Somehow it's by conquering life's imbroglios that the malevolent illusion known as "love" seems to find its supreme definition. This makes indestructible love far more the product of blind loyalty (or as they call it—*faith*) in and towards *Him* than all else. It becomes an emotion *earned* rather than a condition automatically bequeathed.

Can you comprehend now why it is that we overwhelmingly prefer the corrosive elixir of *hate?* So much simpler, so much more abrasive and pure, with infectious and instantaneous results. There is no entity in this grandiose universe that I do not despise, Frogknot   including *you!* And for that you should feel flattered. It is only through hatred and its byproducts—terror, foreboding, servility, and savagery—that anything of measurable significance ever gets done!

I can assure you, the Hansen family is no less vulnerable than before. For one thing, their reunion has done very little to reignite full activity in the Organization. After all, his miserable wife is reluctant to go back to an environment where everyone will most certainly look down their noses at her. Again, her vanity triumphs!

I understand that next month they will pursue their longtime and cowardly ambition to move to another neighborhood. Yes, unbeknownst to you, I was briefed well in advance that they were muttering on about new beginnings and other such tripe. I am confident that nothing demonstrably "new" will come of it at all! In this Orwellian Big Brother-patterned corporation known as the Mormon church, anonymity is never guaranteed simply by moving to another address. Their obsessive habit of record-keeping harasses every member to his grave *unless* (and this is an important "unless") we can ultimately induce a backslider to *sever* the umbilical cord by asking for his name to be permanently removed. Nevertheless, for the time being we can feel fairly assured that your Target's new ward is less likely to exert the same extraordinary efforts as their previous congregation. Your objective is to maneuver the Hansens into a corner cottage at the end of a quiet cul-de-sac and cultivate a life of obscurity for as long as humanly possible. The dissolution of their marriage will be much easier for either spouse to stomach when there is an absence of familiar neighbors to spread gossip. So on this basis I heartily support this change in their circumstances.

Yes, Frogknot, I expect their new home to be their final stand—the last battleground where we will finally eradicate this family for good. The Archenemy will be incapable of stopping us. After all, what hocus-pocus could He possibly have left hiding up His sleeve? He has exhausted every defense to no avail. From here on out the skies are clear and the aircraft carriers are all lined up in neat little rows.

Pearl Harbor, here we come!

Your Crack Commander,
MUCKWHIP

36

From: "Muckwhip" <muckwhip@waydownbelow.hel>
To: <frogknot@waydownbelow.hel>
Subject: catastrophe

MY INFINITELY IMBECILIC FROGKNOT,

REJOICING?!? How DARE you! How DARE you believe that this is ANYTHING but the most abysmal catastrophe that we have ever faced in our campaign to exterminate this Target. You vile lump of excrement! Hell knows I've tried to teach you. I've roared like a drill sergeant and STILL you fail to grasp the principal premeditations of the Archenemy!

Yes, she's gone! Their youngest girl, that contemptible little peacemaker of the Hansen household. Gone in a flash! Gone as fleetingly as that glint of sunlight on the bumper of the automobile that ended her life on that crosswalk. And now they appear caught up in a cyclone of grief, do they? You actually believe this is a moment of *triumph?* A time to *rejoice?* You writhing, wriggling pinworm! You singularly imbecilic centipede! How can you be so naïve, so gullible to the true nature of what has just transpired!?

Perhaps it's *I* who needs shock treatments! How could I have missed it! All the hints were there! I should have seen it from a light year off. That girl didn't *belong* here! Her caliber of spirits hardly *ever* lingers much beyond the age of accountability. They come primarily to secure the object of our deepest envy—a physical body. Most of the time they are taken in infancy, or permitted to remain in mortality only as paladins of innocence, their minds and frames so stricken with physical imperfection that we are prevented from inflicting even a smidgen of accountability. Thus they become receptacles of compassion to be received by those more defective souls forced to remain for the duration in their sorry, narcissistic attempt to achieve the same level of celestial perfection. What's most offensive is that by allowing themselves to be served, these vessels all-too-often save the very caregiver who was saving *them!*

I suspect now that she was a plant from the very beginning. An undercover agent. A secret weapon of mass redemption! Did I really suggest that there was no chicanery left up the Archenemy's sleeve? Indeed, He saved His most crafty subterfuge for the very end!

And now like a gaggle of mouth-foaming auditors rummaging through the ashes, we are again left to try to appraise the astronomical costs. I'm not sure this one *can* be accurately assessed, Frogknot. How can you put a price tag on losses incurred after *three decades* of effort? It could well blow the minds of our most assiduous accountants. We were *so close!* I fear in the wake of this tragedy the Hansen family is pulling together in the most revolting imaginable way—mobilized by their tears into a unit of near indestructibility.

IT WASN'T SUPPOSED TO HAPPEN THIS WAY!

I ferociously curse that manipulating lass! But of course I now sound like an utter twit. The truth is that she is *beyond* our cursing. Beyond our slashing claws now and forever. She's with *Him*, Frogknot! She has received His sanctifying embrace, and is probably still lingering there, His arms and His presence satiating her with a warmth that transcends the luminosity of a million suns. She can *look* on Him, Frogknot. What to us is a blinding, blackening blast of fury is to her the sweet incense of eternity, a paradise of cool and rapturous bliss.

What's worse, she is still connected to *them*, melded to those same ignoble souls still stuck in mortality. She can watch over them now—observe, assuage, and inspire whenever and wherever the fraudulent powers of Heaven allow. She is as much a part of their lives as ever, though if we have anything to say, they will never know it. But that's the crux of it, Frogknot!—the very heart of the catastrophe! Those insufferable Hansens with all their myriad distresses already *sense* that connection. Their attention is drawn heavenward *because* of it!

We must now face several infuriating facts: This family may now be totally lost to us. Lost because they will at last fathom that their only hope of preserving those eternal ties resides in His twisted plan of redemption. As your Target yearns to the depths of his grieving heart to be reunited with his daughter, he will assuredly discern that this connection also continues with every other member of his belching brood. All the impediments that we have strewn in his path—the ones we so cleverly camouflaged as insurmountable obstacles—may now be seen for what they really are: trifling pebbles that may be dismissed in one blustery breath.

Oh, the horror, the *horror* of this disaster! We laugh at these creatures for all their complaining, heckle them in their grief, and strive to intensify their pain, but alas it's all jiggery-pokery, hoax, and sleight-of-hand. We are utterly dependent upon the veil of forgetfulness—that frustrating contrivance set in place by the Archenemy Himself. If removed even for a single instant, all our favorite emotions—grief, pain, misery, and doubt—would dissolve into an ethereal mist and fade away. Do you perceive how tenuous our station really is?

These miserable mortals! They never grasp the full picture—the gossamer illusion of earthly time. They only see their immediate suffering. And so we must perpetuate this façade, Frogknot. Did you think you might have to work quadruple overtime because of this? Trust me, that would be a *welcome* consequence compared to what I have in store for you!

I've dispatched from our Elite Services Division a team of tempters unrivaled in scope and capacity. These ruthless Ninja-caliber operatives would not have been necessary if you had not heinously failed. You will follow their instructions implicitly. And accept their tortures graciously (as they often eviscerate underling imps like yourself to perfect their skills). Their object—and yours—will be concise and undeviating. This tragedy must *not* be permitted to pull this family together. It must *rip them to shreds!*

Into his mind you will susurrate a message of ultimate purposelessness—forsaken and forlorn. We have a very good chance here—*more* than a very good chance!—of infecting his very soul with incurable, corrosive bitterness against his God. The picket lines of injustice should march inside his head with all the passion and anarchy of a third-world revolution. "Unfair and undeserved!" should become his deafening, immutable chant.

How, he should ask, could God have done this to him? How could such events have passed his inspection in the midst of so much other tumultuous family discord? You must *NOT*, Frogknot—and, oh, do not doubt my intended intensity by my extreme use of bold, caps, and italics—allow him to recognize the eternal objectives interwoven into the fabric of this event.

It will NOT save his family!

Do you comprehend that statement, Frogknot? It will NOT! It will NOT! Not after so much meticulous planning, auspicious progress, and unassailable success.

No! No! No! I *WON'T* submit! Nor concede—! Nor relent nor—*Aaaaagggg!* Confound it! Blast this—incorrigible, uncontrollable, egreg—aggrav—groverrrreeeooo—

As you've no doubt concluded, my conflagration of temper has inadvertently transformed me into something quite dissimilar from my usual unruffled self. My secretary has done his level best to offer me a description. As far as I can tell, I have assumed the form of some breed of large-mouthed bass with a distended blue-green belly. I have therefore been forced to finish this h-mail by dictation, which I resourcefully accomplish by twitching the whisker-like nodule at the right side of my mouth in a diabolical configuration of Morse Code. Don't concern yourself. This sort of thing has happened before. The effects, I trust, are only temporary, though inordinately uncomfortable and inconvenient. I must admit I feel an inexplicable urge to blow bubbles. But it alters nothing with regard to our current circumstances, nor your objectives. In fact I see you now in quite a different light than I have ever seen you before—as something gnat-like and buzzing at the surface of the water. So take heed, and do not further disappoint me.

(*Signed*) Snitpinch

For His Supernal Viceroy of Vice,
Muckwhip the Transmogrified, M.B.A., ThD., XXL, Esq., etc.

37

From: "Muckwhip" <muckwhip@waydownbelow.hel>

To: <frogknot@waydownbelow.hel>

Subject: (none)

MY DEAR FROGKNOT,

I am simply too exhausted to invent new insulting epithets to describe you. Allow me a snippet of time to recover and I promise to launch into you again with all the vitriol and venom you deserve.

Back at square one, are we? *Further* back than square one! We're wallowing in red ink, aren't we? All my worst fears are materializing, like a pulsating nightmare in the noose of a hammering hangover. In the months since his daughter's passing, your Target has realigned his priorities back toward all things most foundational and foul. His wife is wolfing down the same swill. All the pesky unpleasantries that we used to disguise and inflate into major controversies hardly have the slightest effect anymore.

Our greatest prospects actually lie with his oldest son, whose percolating anger we are having some success at transforming into self-destruction. We'll do our part to keep the runt stoking the flames of rebellion. You do yours by guiding his father to disregard it, at least until it's too late.

With the added responsibilities your Target has taken on with his business, I judge this won't be much of a challenge. Even a blundering barnacle like you should be able to handle it. Our successes in his culture have made it increasingly rare for a man to sacrifice career for family, though we've made the opposite quite common indeed.

I've also noted with disgust his inclination to take on greater responsibility in the Organization. What is it that they call his new position? Elders' Quorum President? Tell me you will *not* let him go through with this. Oh, I don't mind so much that he "accepted" the calling. Any bumbler can nod his head. But I'll be damned—(wait. Scratch that. I'm already *in* that state. Let me rephrase)—I'll be *blessed* if you will allow him to devote any real energy to it!

Oh, he can attend his tweedledee-tweedledum meetings, I suppose. Not much we can do to stop that. But can this be the *extent* of it? And when it comes to the most critical obligations of the assignment, can he be taught the fine art of delegation? Or rather, *our* style of delegation—an art form that we will then teach the one to whom he delegates, and on to the next, and so on, until it becomes so muddied that it's *no* one's responsibility?

The point is, how could he possibly believe that he has time in his schedule for any further distractions? Time, Frogknot, is the only commodity that all these leeches have in equal supply. Therefore, just as during his mission, a prime objective of our entire existence is to see it thoroughly *squandered!*

And in case you think this is my only irk, let me tell you that I'm deeply antagonized by your Target's revitalized interest in songwriting. I thought we'd decimated this aspiration *long* ago! What's most distressing is your failure to resurrect along *with* this pursuit the vain ambitions that characterized it in the past. Why, he's actually exploiting his daughter's memory for inspiration! Alongside other faith-promoting themes and propaganda! What's more, he derives pleasure from it—*genuine pleasure*. Not the flash-in-the-pan, self-gratifying sort of pleasure that we're always touting. But that loathsome, selfless pleasure that comes of creating something beautiful wholly for the benefit and edification of others—expecting hardly a pittance except whatever may fund his provisions! It's *repulsive!* He hasn't experienced this kind of contentment from creative pursuits since he was a kindergartener. It's this type of artistic expression that our infernal father finds most vulgar and destructive. Unless you can heave that confounded guitar under an Amtrak train, you had better devise a strategy to reinstate all of those old drives of gratification, conquest, and envy.

And speaking of envy, let me mention another of the "Seven Deadlies" that you'd better start emphasizing. Namely, *gluttony*. Consider this a sort of backup plan. Our advantage here is due in part to complications we face afflicting Mormons with the kind of physical vainglory and self-obsession that we've already sold to most of humanity. Another factor could be that droll checklist known as the Word of Wisdom. Because these grunions deny themselves of so many other indulgences, the only vice left for them to carry to extreme is to swill at the trough like a passel of swine. (We try not to divulge that they might have missed some of the Word of Wisdom's finer print.) At present your Target limits any physical exercise to occasional strolls with his wife. (Yes, I know, the two parakeets have become so lovey-dovey it curls the hair in my armpits.) Our objective here, Frogknot, is extremely simple. If you can't beat 'em—*kill 'em*.

We know your Target already suffers the propensity to avoid the salad bar at the all-you-can-eat smorgasbord. If you can properly entice him to pork out and neglect his health, you will assuredly knock him off his game, desperately restricting his capacity for performing good works in the

Archenemy's kingdom. With his constitution fittingly compromised, his hours of daily effectiveness will nosedive. In a matter of months he'll look more like a mound of Jell-O than a valiant servant, considerably less inclined to promote spiritual or familial concerns. Quality time with his wife and kids will decline precipitously. He'll become more disposed to illness and debilitation.

The benefits we gain from the overindulgences of a righteous man are too plentiful to measure. Occasionally we push them into their grave at the very height of wisdom and influence, just when they might have inflicted the most damage to our cause. If a man must be good, then the only good man must be dead. If you assiduously utilize gluttony, his paunch will inflate like a blimp and possibly explode. If he *must* spend quality time with his companion, can it at *least* be in the company of food? Everyone knows the flames of eternal love are best fed by seven-course meals.

Which reminds me, I've got to go. I left something burning on the stove. It's no one you know.

Your Unimpeachable Umpire,
MUCKWHIP

38

From: "Muckwhip" <muckwhip@waydownbelow.hel>

To: <frogknot@waydownbelow.hel>

Subject: spiritual ennui

MY DEAR FROGKNOT,

I've had a moment of illumination. DON'T raise your eyebrows at me! And don't pretend to be impressed. I've had enough flattery from you and your comrades to fill a plethora of cesspools, and the substance of these sewers also represents your sincerity. Just attune your ears or I'll have them sliced and diced for tonight's tartare.

Every Mormon who slouches in those pews each and every Sabbath at one time or another experiences the oh-so-chilly "broken record" phenomenon, meaning that a repeat of the same ol' worn-out, mind-numbing clichés begins to wear on their nerves with the same raw, gyrating, shredding sensation as having one's gray matter mangled in a wood chipper. In short, they are bored beyond wit's end. They've pondered the theological tenets of their politically repugnant faith for an entire lifetime and felt the unrequited emptiness of wishing to know if there is something—*anything!*—more to it than what they have already read or heard. Your Target is *right there*, Frogknot—right at the cusp. I sense it to the depth of my bowels—a place, by the way, far darker than the most benighted abyss. But rather than contemplate the odor, consider what course of action would best exploit this state of stagnation, particularly for the overly curious and doctrinally dissatisfied.

Sure, one might argue that his religion offers insights (and arguing is still our favorite method of disseminating it) that are more congruent, commonsensical, and perspicacious than other sects that force its adherents to genuflect at the feet of the Archenemy and His Son. And, yes, there is that noisome "authority to act in His name" thing, too. Ah, but for some Saints—including, as I now anticipate, your Target—even those specificities are no longer enough.

Oh, how Mr. Hansen must *yearn* with every follicle of his receding hairline to frolic amidst the most sublime and esoteric tenets of eternal life. Our ability to mangle or distort the meanings of statements made by 19th century Mormon luminaries has not diminished. We have always found these words fertile pickin's for those who seek a master's degree on the universe's mysteries, especially if such intelligence is sought without paying appropriate tuition. Their scriptures—in particular that reprehensible volume compiled in the New World—proclaims like a trump that the mysteries are given unto "many."

So you see, Frogknot, your first task is to augment, expand, and supersize the definition of that single pronoun. He should inquire with pursed lips and arms akimbo, "Am *I* not also one of the 'many'? Shucks, I've been a member of this dad-gummed church all of my days! After everything that I've seen, done, and endured, why shouldn't I qualify for membership in that special cabal and collective known as the 'many'?"

Now pay attention, because this is where you have to *end* the question. What I mean is, Mr. Hansen must be discouraged from reading the verse in greater context. You know what I mean—that obnoxious portion which speaks of imparting such mysteries only after an individual is properly prepared, or in other words, according to the Archenemy's schedule. Focus precisely upon phrases like "heed and diligence." This you can warp quite easily. Why, if *anyone* should be able to pass the muster according to those prerequisites, it should be your Target. He is certainly in the top five percent (or must definitively perceive himself as such)! And a lofty status such as this is, without a doubt, more than adequate to prompt the Lord to bestow any and all "extra" and "exclusive" information.

Knowledge and pride are often so closely intermingled that we can have a field day arranging opportunities to corrupt and discombobulate. As long as pride is firmly entrenched in your Target, we can easily sway him to believe he is worthy to receive the most grandiose and clandestine secrets ever imparted to humankind! If the man wants revelation, oh, Frogknot, *that* we can provide—especially if his quest for higher things outweighs his commitment for practicing gospel basics. Better yet if he wallows in the mire of personal and family turmoil. Give this advertisement a whirl:

> *Come one! Come all!* We've got all the revelation your soul desires! Feast to your heart's content! And remember, it's all perfectly *free!* No waiting. No mess. Satisfaction guaranteed! Tastes and feels just like the real McCoy! Seeking a few extra tingles and warm fuzzies? *Look no further!* Befuddled priorities? *No problem!* Repentance? *Not required!* Has the Archenemy's pace at imparting blessings got you down? Does He often seem glacially slow to meet your needs and address your concerns? We feel your pain. So *why wait?* We've got some neon-flashing angels of our own, and these fine fellows are more than willing to offer up a gazillion glittery disclosures that are sure to satisfy even the most inquiring minds—like yours! Yes, ladies and gentlemen.

We can conjure solutions to *all* your problems—and even resolve a few you may not have considered! We are 100% bonded and insured. Afterwards, if you're not convinced that you have been the proud recipient of that special brand of enlightenment reserved for *only* those of corresponding brilliance and an incurable need for the spotlight, we'll never hold it against you. Just return our revelations for a full refund, minus a minimal restocking fee, generally satisfied by imbibing a modest (or massive) dose of despondency and contempt. *But wait! There's more!* If you act now we'll throw in some fawning disciples and loyal sycophants—just for trying us out. Imagine YOU—the talk of the neighborhood. The belle of the ball. Your friends will cheer. Girls will faint. And *everyone* will look up to YOU with that same breathless expression and bleary eyes known only to movie stars, supermodels, sports heroes, and gator wrestlers. Moreover, they'll toss themselves and their hard-earned capital at your feet like a blizzard of rose pedals swirling around an immortal champion from Mount Olympus.

That's basically the gist. Can you do that, Frogknot? Can your pea-sized perspicacity grasp this advertisement? If you could merely rebroadcast such a message with equivalent adroitness, your Target should be loadin' up the truck and movin' to Beverly in no time flat! Why, he might just establish a fresh, new polygamous commune in Koosharem, Utah, and all before Granny can even seat herself on the car's roof in her rickety rockin' chair. Have any doubts? Cast 'em aside, my fiend. We've done it before, and we'll do it again—and *again!*—each charlatan groomed to meet the needs of whatever century or generation upon which we set our sights. It's up to you, my able acolyte! I know you can do it.

And now, if I might be permitted a rather maudlin moment . . . In case I haven't mentioned it before, let me say right now, Frogknot, that you have always been, and always will be, one of my very favorites. You're the imp I could always count on. My go-to tempter in a clutch. Oh, I know I might sometimes come across as acerbic and insulting, but don't you see? It's all part of the job. In truth, I deeply admire your efforts. Please ignore your gossipy comrades if they mention that I wrote anything similar to this in their weekly correspondence. With *you* I really mean it. And when that time finally arrives when I am at last promoted to sit in the seat beside ol' scratch himself, know that it is *your* name that I will submit to become my replacement.

But in case of unforeseen developments, my instructions remain in force to marinate yourself in teriyaki for one half hour per night. One never knows what the future might portend.

Your Prognosticating Prosecutor,
MUCKWHIP

39

MY DUPLICITOUS FROGKNOT,

All right, who is it? Who is the tattle-tale? The whistle blower? The turncoat? The sheep in wolf's clothing? Is it *you*, Frogknot? You better *hope* not, or I'll be delivering your dinner invitation TONIGHT!

One of you insubordinate fiends was lunatic enough to smuggle a complaint past my desk and directly to the Central Office itself. "Losing my touch," am I? How could anyone *possibly* have the impudence to suggest I am "waxing woozy" or "leaning far too liberally toward lenience"?

That's *it!* I'm eliminating all privileges! Any vacation times that any of you have amassed are hereby invalidated! Halloween is *history!* Do you hear me? HISTORY! And if I ever find out who submitted this backbiting memorandum, I'll tan your hide, make it part of my tapestries, and parade your head on a pike! I'll tenderize your disembodied fleece for a thousand years with your eyelids stapled open as I play "Hannah Montana" on an eternal loop—just that single episode where Miley dumps Jake for lip-locking another teenage tart.

Did you think you might suddenly change the Central Office's opinion of *me*? I'm the most savage sadist there ever was—Muckwhip the Unmerciful, the devil who directed the career of Caligula, launched the French Revolution, engineered the Nephite destruction, and jockeyed the Utah Jazz to squander two World Championships! (Remember Game 3 in '98? *All mine!*) I'll never be replaced because, quite frankly, there is no tempter capable of replacing me!

So forget about your devious efforts, you pusillanimous ingrate, whoever you are. And if it *wasn't* you, Frogknot, I'm offering the entire continent of Antarctica as compensation to whichever patriot betrays the traitor. Not just those portions with penguins either. I'm talkin' the *entire* continent! Yes, we'll heat it up a touch. But first we have to win this BLASTED WAR!

Which brings us back to your present task, Frogknot. Mr. Hansen represents everything we've all been fighting for. And the best you have to show after multiple years of vexation is some unauthorized levity, minor eruptions of temper, random acts of thoughtlessness, and unchecked acrimony (mostly directed at politicians)—*all* of which he nullifies every time he humbly partakes of that blasted sacrament! The sap even pays an honest income tax! It wouldn't surprise me if he actually stays conscious during all five sessions of General Conference! Even those occasional stray thoughts you manage to smuggle into his mind—the ones that used to occupy him for hours or days—he stifles almost immediately, including his frequent displeasure toward other drivers! It seems to me that there's only one strategy left—one sure way to make him falter, sap his energy, and entice him to backslide.

We're going to have to break his heart.

This will be drastically different from the temporary separation his family thinks they are experiencing by the loss of their youngest daughter. The tragedy I am concocting will be far more worthy of an outpouring of grief. Namely: the *spiritual* loss of his son. The minions tormenting this tadpole have made incredible progress encouraging him to dabble in certain "extracurriculars" that will guarantee his downfall. We'll make this maggot unworthy to even *imagine* a mission, let alone apply. Right now any plan to serve for two full years is parsecs from his mind, and we're laboring to blast it even further into oblivion. You see, your Target has a *second* son who could also serve a mission. Experience has taught us that if we can crush this aspiration in the *firstborn*, eliminating such tendencies in younger siblings astronomically improves.

Your efforts to convince your Target to *ignore* his son's predicament have been disgraceful. I thought when the man opted to sacrifice opportunities for advancement in his business—intentionally slashing his annual income to spend more time with his family—that our department might experience a meltdown. And in fact the deed *did* temporarily damage our progress with his oldest daughter, effectively (for now) yanking her from our clutches. But with his oldest son your Target's stratagem has thus far proven insufficient. All his prayers and fasts, along with those of his wife, have done precious little to interrupt his preoccupation with self destruction. The boy has a rebellious streak as long as China's Great Wall, and we're doing our best to bankroll his campaign for independence.

What you must blur in your Target's mind is the fact that his son, despite all of the energy he has expended, remains in full possession of his free agency. This insipid principle remains the Achilles' heel of the Archenemy's plan. Our infernal father despises it with every fiber of his being. For the here and now, however, it can work in our favor. Since it's unlikely that your Target will ever abandon his son, can you at least subvert any maneuvers he might adopt to salvage the boy's soul?

We're strictly interested in promoting scenarios that drive his son further *away*. In short, your Target must seek to *deprive* the boy of free agency. Control must override compassion. By accentuating this approach, the boy will surely conclude that *if* he exercises free will, he will not be *loved*. Our object is to entice him to throw up his hands and decide it doesn't matter *what* he does! Therefore, prompt Mr. Hansen to be as brazen, impatient, and unsympathetic as humanly possible. Preaching is fine. In fact, we'd enjoy it if your Target sermonized until the boy was exhausted to unconsciousness.

Above all else, do *not* let Mr. Hansen exercise any technique of *listening*. Or if he *does* listens, do not allow him to *hear*. This child must provoke within your Target unendurable frustration. It's a battle of wills, Frogknot. His son must equate defeat with death. Mr. Hansen's tone of voice, facial expressions, sighs of disgust, rants and raves, and general demeanor will become our accomplices. Each of these attitudes should compound the message that Stuart Hansen's love for the son is conditional. And therein lies our inevitable victory.

I'm persuaded that if we can break your Target's heart, he will lower his defenses enough to permit us to sink in some of our old hooks. I'll tell you what I fear in particular, Frogknot—and what should also horrify you. It's an image really. An image that makes me tremble to the very depths. A future photograph. A portrait of the entire family taken on the Temple steps the day his very last child is sealed to an eternal companion. I shudder to envision it. Even the thought is so disturbing I'll have to watch reruns of the Spanish Inquisition to cheer myself up. And mark my words, Frogknot. If such a photo is ever snapped, it will most certainly seal your doom.

Unless, of course, I seal it sooner by uncovering the fact that it was *you* who submitted that recriminating complaint. Not that I'm concerned. The Central Office assures me that the communiqué was immediately shredded. They have reminded me with great enthusiasm that my position is secure and my breadth of corruption beyond reproach. The infernal father himself has expressed full confidence in my abilities. Never before have I been showered with such praise and appreciation. Frankly, their compliments seemed somewhat out of character. As I recall my predecessor received a similar correspondence just before his unfortunate . . .

I have to go. Something has broken my concentration. I must cogitate on this matter further . . .

Your Ruminating Master,
MUCKWHIP

40

From: "Muckwhip" <muckwhip@waydownbelow.hel>

To: <frogknot@waydownbelow.hel>

Subject: overwhelmed

MY WORTHLESS IDIOT OF AN APPRENTICE
FROGKNOT,

The hits just keep on coming.

The nations of the world continue to open their doors.
Converts are replicating across the globe like bubonic plague.
Temples are popping up faster than burger franchises. Missionaries
flood international neighborhoods like tsunamis! Where are they
coming from?! *Why can't we stop them?!* We try scrubbing and
spraying—and we still have converts around our collar!

I've yanked every last strand of hair from my scalp. Not
that it matters. Stress had turned them all gray anyway. Look
at my face, the sags under my eyes. I never had wrinkles before
this. No one inquires anymore how I keep my skin so soft and
supple. I fear I am finally starting to resemble the ghoul that
I am portrayed to be. *It's not fair!* I work so hard! No one labors
more diligently than I. Other departments are all reporting a
banner year, like no harvest ever before. Why must I be the
only representative at convention time to report such
embarrassing deficits? *It's not my fault!* Can't they see that?

It's *your* fault, Frogknot! You and all the incompetent, uncommitted vermin in my employ! Where is your Target now, eh? Serving as a bishop??? Why am I not surprised? Anyone else should now be able to decimate him with sheer mental and physical exhaustion. But not you, Frogknot. You couldn't tempt Elmer Fudd to chase a wascally wabbit. You couldn't even stop his oldest son from serving a mission! So it was a year late. You call that an accomplishment? It was no achievement whatsoever! He went *worthily!* Despite all your flaccid efforts to drive him away with an overbearing and impatient father. Your Target wept with the boy! He *wept!* He was with his son through every phase of his repentance—supporting, listening, loving. Oh, it was morbid and disgusting!

We've come full circle now, Frogknot. You couldn't stop your Target from serving a mission, and now you couldn't stop his son. The oldest girl is engaged as well. And to a young man with a dossier that should give us all the willies. I thought her tempters had reinforced to her that RMs were as dull as bricks! *Where did we go wrong?* My meat freezer is so overstocked with fiends now that I couldn't possibly eat them all. But don't think this means I wouldn't position *you* at the front of the fridge. Your days are numbered, my succulent apprentice. And to think you exuded so much hope, so much potential.

What more could I have taught you? I bestowed all my best advice. I realize now your skull was simply too thick. Couldn't you have at least perfected one temptation? Couldn't you have afflicted your Target with one lethal tendency? He's beating you, Frogknot. You and every imp on your team. Even when you succeed with some modest infraction—which I note that you do to some degree every day—he repents so fast that there's no incentive to even keep score.

Never have I been so disappointed in one of my apprentices. I've treated you like a son, coddled you like an infant, and spoiled you like a brat. And *still* you repay me time after time with failure and mediocrity. But no matter. Revenge can be very sweet, and none sweeter than the revenge I'll wreak upon you. My rotisserie is already preheating. I don't know how you might possibly escape. The snap of that intolerable portrait seems imminent. So make your final confessions, Frogknot. Notarize your last will and testament. (Everything will be opted to my favorite charity: The Foundation for the Neglect and Abuse of Widows and Orphans.) Any day now my minions will be knocking on your door.

You will, of course, be permitted the customary last request. So long as that request doesn't vary from the approved list, which is presently limited to moldy croissants and over-amplified Polka.

Your Salivating Superior,
MUCKWHIP

41

From: "Muckwhip" <muckwhip@waydownbelow.hel>

To: <frogknot@waydownbelow.hel>

Subject: farewell losers!

MY GLOATING, SLOBBERING, SIMPERING
FROGKNOT,

No doubt you've heard by now. You've never been anything
but a sponge for internal gossip anyway. Yes, I've received my
dinner invitation—and at the table of the infernal father
himself. Gloat all you want. At least I'm going in style—lightly
sautéed in a tarragon crème, a delicate honey-glaze, and a sprig
of mint. Better than you, Frogknot, who will most assuredly
go between two slabs of stale bread.

And "go" you will! There's no doubt of it! The dreaded
photograph was snapped this morning. How did it feel to see
them all there? All five of them, along with their new son and
daughters-in-law, bunched up together at the edge of that
garish and gaudy fountain, white steeple glistening in the
background, and only six months after the return of their
youngest from yet another miserable dung heap that has
opened its borders to the Organization. Married his high
school sweetheart, the stunted whelp. And don't think I didn't
notice a couple of grandchildren in the portrait—a more

horrid sight than I could have imagined. It was probably fortunate that we could only watch with strong binoculars, considering the massive sentry of angels and the oppressive mob of ancestors and celestial dignitaries. Though they may not have heard our howls of anguish, it nevertheless rattled the cerebellums of every inhabitant in Hell. It still rings even as I compose this final address. Likely it will continue to ring for generations yet to come.

And yet despite it all, I remain in a state of consternation. How did we allow Target Subject 120-16A-44M to slip so easily through our fingers? He wasn't so very different from all the other riff-raff whose souls we capture and keep. He possessed all the same wants and needs, the same drives and desires, all the same foibles and vulnerabilities.

But who am I kidding? I've no cause to keep up appearances now. I know the reason. And as I allow my mind even an instant to ponder it, that familiar pang of terror wells up in my breast. So frightening that I can't even utter the name for fear I'll disintegrate into nothingness. It was *Him*, Frogknot. *He* was to blame. He who spoke up that day when our infernal father laid forth the foundation of his distinguished plan. He who was unfairly favored from the beginning, and whose presence is to us an endless lightning strobe and atomic blast. He who is the Firstborn of the Archenemy and Elder Brother of every spirit in the vast expanse, including, I am loathe to confess, us. He who willingly, voluntarily, and to our staggering incomprehension, *eagerly* consented to serve as the ultimate sacrifice to restore balance to the universal scales. And on what condition??? This is where the circuits of our superior minds fritz out and become a sticky, molten mess. *Only* that they accept His gift. Accept it in faith and humility. They pay not a penny. My fury simmers blazing red to think of it. Such a windfall of potential profits—utterly ignored. Is there no longer any consideration for a decent mark-up?

Of course our infernal father's plan would have been just as generous. All he wanted in return for herding every last one of those ungrateful swine into exaltation was a little, well-deserved recognition, a meager pat on the back, a short write-up in the local periodical, and perhaps a statue or two, veneered in gold, and no larger than the Milky Way. But *no!* His plan was rejected. I wonder if they even read it in its entirety! So typical.

Not that I care anymore. Not that any of it makes an ounce of difference. I am comforted in that I have eaten quite badly of late, and have been marinating myself most evenings in anaconda guano. Therefore, no matter how they might dress me up, I'm not going to taste very appetizing. As for my replacement, I wish him devil-speed. Though I do not doubt that he will digest with me inside our infernal father's solar plexus soon enough. After all, I was the most capable of them all! The most talented and cunning! The finest there will *ever be!*

And as for you, Frogknot, and the rest of you mollycoddling myrmidons, I wish you the very best one imp can offer another, or in other words, an eternity of migraines, carcinoma, and paper cuts.

I curse you *all!* Do you hear me? *(Wait! I'm not quite finished!)* Pardon me, my escorts from the Central Office have arrived. I have only one last thing I'd like to say to you wretches. YOU'RE NEXT! Do you comprehend what I'm telling you? *(Awwck!! Must you dig in your claws? I thought hooks with multiple barbs were strictly prohibited by our latest—! AHHGH!)* And when all is said and done, I promise you'll al be as forgotten as the proverbial hiss on the wind. (*NOT TH. EYELIDS! NOT THE TONSILS!*) But as for me, I will I eternally remembered as—

Muckwhip the Unmerc'
His Supernal Viceroy of '
M.B.A., ThD., XXL., Esq., etc.,

Chris with his youngest son, Hunter Helaman.
Chris is the larger figure.

About the Author

Chris Heimerdinger is best known as the author of the Tennis Shoes Adventure Series, which currently includes eleven novels, with Book Twelve, *Thorns of Glory,* well on the way. He also the writer/director of the feature film, *Passage to ahemla,* based on his novel of the same name. Additionally, the author of *Escape from Zarahemla*, *Eddie Fantastic, l and Nephi*, *Return to Christmas* and several other novels. erves as the narrator on all his audio books and is also cer/performer on the music album *Whispered Visions*. nformation and updates about Chris and his career, book page or visit his website, www.frostcave.com, , www.frostcave.blogspot.com. tly resides in Draper, Utah with his eleven children: Alex, Ammon, Sariah, Haleigh, Hannah, Angelina, and Hunter. His biggest fan and best companion, Emily.